Harlequin ◆ Romances

OTHER
Harlequin Romances
by MARY WIBBERLEY

The Moon-dancers

by

MARY WIBBERLEY

Harlequin Books

TORONTO • LONDON • NEW YORK • AMSTERDAM • SYDNEY • WINNIPEG

Original hardcover edition published in 1976
by Mills & Boon Limited

ISBN 0-373-02031-7

Harlequin edition published December 1976

Printed in U.S.A.

CHAPTER ONE

LORY STEVENSON took a last brief look at herself in her handbag mirror, and then put it away. She didn't allow herself a small smile—there were others on the plane, and they might wonder at it. She felt like a spy going into enemy territory, which was absurd, but at the same time, that thought added a touch of zest to what she was about to do.

Her mind went back to the last conversation with her father, as she had been about to leave London Airport on the first stage of her journey.

'Got everything?' he'd asked, then before she could reply, 'God, but I wouldn't recognize you as my daughter. You look almost *plain*!'

'Thanks,' she had murmured dryly. 'Considering it's taken me the best part of an hour to achieve the result, I'll take it as a compliment.' And she had caught a glimpse of herself then, in the darkened glass at the end of a cigarette kiosk, and known what he had meant. Her rich dark hair was scraped back into a very unflattering bun, and she wore no make-up, not even a vestige of lipstick. The trouble was, there wasn't much you could do to disguise a pert tip-tilted nose or sooty-lashed eyes, but she had done her best with a pair of granny glasses with plain lenses, and these she wore perched on the end of that nose. Flat brogues, tweed skirt and figure-concealing thick sweater—all in a disgusting shade of anonymous brown—completed her outfit.

'Ugh!' she said. 'I haven't overdone it, have I?'

Her father could scarcely conceal laughter. 'No. I'd like to see old Mackinnon's face when you roll up at the guest-house, though. You must phone me after you're settled in, let me know. Got all your books and papers?'

Lory patted the briefcase—brown, of course—which she carried together with her suitcase. 'All here.' Something was disturbing her, but she didn't realize what it was until her father had gone, a few minutes later, and she was making her way to the plane that was to take her to Glasgow. Nobody had given her a second glance—or even a first one, come to that. And she wasn't used to it. She was accustomed to drawing stares of open admiration from practically every male who came within seeing distance, wherever she went. She had been used to that state of affairs ever since the age of fifteen, and now, eight years later, it was something of a shock to realize that she might have been invisible for all the notice anyone was taking.

'Good,' she thought, for she was not a girl to dwell on negative thoughts. 'That should provide me with some material for an article at some future date.' And then she dismissed the uneasiness from her, for there were more immediate concerns on her mind.

And these concerns came back to her as she looked out of the window of the small plane after that final look in her handbag mirror. She was embarking on a deliberate deception, and the fact that it was from the highest motives did not stop the faint twinge of unease that assailed her. If old Mackinnon—she could never think of him as anything else after her father's vivid description of the elderly Scots woman-hater who owned the island of Creagdubh, her destination—found out what she was really doing there, she didn't doubt that she would be thrown off immediately. She sighed. And yet her work would surely help him and his islanders. Why were some people so resistant to progress?

The island stretched out below her, a dark jewel in the sea, pounded by the wild waves, for she could feel the wind buffeting the plane, and she saw the rugged beauty of it—and yet knew that life there was hard. You could not live off beauty alone. She patted the briefcase on her knee. In it was a small storehouse of information, a dossier to be studied in relation to her work on Creagdubh—and not to be seen by anyone else.

She closed her eyes and lay back in her seat. She had had a chance to look at her fellow passengers when they embarked at Glasgow. It was almost certain that they would be going to Creagdubh House as well, for it was the only guest-house on the island, and they didn't look like natives. There were four women and two men, all middle-aged, and one of the women had smiled and nodded shyly at Lory as they waited to board the plane. Lory sighed. If they were all experienced ornithologists she would have to be careful—although that was a minor problem. If people thought you were a beginner they were only too willing to help and advise. No, the major problem was finding sufficient time to be on her own to do the work she was really here for.

She made sure that her seat belt was fastened as the plane circled preparatory to landing. Time would tell. All she wanted was a good meal. She wondered what sort of host old Mackinnon made.

'Excuse me.' She looked up, then round as the voice came from the other side of the aisle. It was the woman who had smiled at Glasgow Airport. 'But are you staying at Creagdubh House as well?'

'Yes,' Lory smiled. 'I take it you are?'

'Yes. Er—is it your first time?'

'It is,' admitted Lory. 'You've been before?' She should have thought. All this time wasted when she could have been finding out about the island, discovering what the place was really like—what kind of life the islanders led, if old Mackinnon was such a dragon——

'Oh, several times. But I thought—well—that you looked like a stranger to these parts. You don't mind me speaking to you? Only everyone at the guest-house is so friendly——'

'Heavens no,' Lory laughed. 'I'm delighted. It's always a little lonely when you go to a strange place for the first

7

time. As a matter of fact I was wondering just what the guest-house is like. The owner—a Mr. Mackinnon, isn't it?—is he the typical Scots host? I've heard *so* much about Scottish hospitality——' and she sighed gently, wistfully, as if to say: I can't wait to taste the food.

The woman laughed. 'Oh yes, he's fine—doesn't say a lot, you understand, but makes everyone very welcome. He's a bit shy, I'd say.'

Shy? Old Mackinnon shy? Hmm, well that was possible, Lory supposed.

'And the food? I suppose it's all home-grown stuff?'

'Oh yes. He's very proud of his vegetable gardens—though how he manages to grow things in the strong sea winds is a miracle. He'll show you round if you ask him, I dare say.'

That was another surprise. Lory's father hadn't exactly said the old man was confined to the house, but she had received that impression, and he must be nearly eighty now. 'Oh, so he's active, is he?' she tried—but clearly failed—to keep the astonishment from her voice, and saw the woman look at her oddly. She found out why a moment later.

'Er—you're not thinking he's *old*, are you?'

'Well, yes! Isn't he?'

But they were landing, and the words were lost in the extra loud roar from the engines as they taxied to a halt on a sparse landing strip, and Lory was left for a few minutes to wait, and wonder.

Silence settled on the plane as the engine coughed and died, and there was a bustle and noise as they all undid seat belts and stood up and stretched, and the woman touched Lory's arm.

'You must be thinking of Mackinnon's great-uncle. I met him once——' and she paused, and smiled, as if she would say too much if she continued.

'Come on, dear, we'll talk outside. My name's Edna Jackson, by the way. I'll introduce you to my sister in a minute.'

They were the last to leave the plane, and as Lory scrambled down on to the pitted tarmac, she instinctively put her hand to her hair to check that the bun was in place. A mischievous wind teased them, and the woman laughed and said: 'It's always breezy here, you'll find.' She drew her companion nearer. 'This is my sister Joan.'

'And I'm Lory Stevenson.' Lory shook hands with them, and smiled. 'Are you—twins?' It seemed an obvious question. Both were clad in similar clothes—sensible tweedy clothes—and had the same round pleasant faces.

Edna nodded. 'Aye, we are. Both widows. We've been coming here for about three years, and look forward to coming, don't we, Joan?'

Joan nodded. 'We do that. Have you come on holiday, love, or have you any special interest in the place?'

This was the first test. Time for the first deception. Lory smiled gently. 'A holiday,' she said, 'but I've heard this place is a bird sanctuary too and—well, I'm only a beginner——' she paused, waiting.

'You are? Lovely!' Edna's face lit up with her smile. 'We'll help you, won't we, Joan?'

'Of course. It's a paradise for bird-lovers, is Creag-dubh—do you know what the name means?'

It was nice to give a completely honest answer. 'No,' Lory admitted. 'It's a Gaelic word, isn't it?'

'Yes. It means Black Rock. And you can see why, when you look out from the plane.'

A Range-Rover was approaching from the distance, and Joan turned to her sister, and then to the others, who stood chatting nearby to the pilot of the plane. 'He's here!' she called, as if they might not have noticed, and then she added: 'Come and meet our new visitor.'

Lory tried—with difficulty—to look shy and diffident, although she was beginning to find, much to her surprise, that the drab clothes she was wearing were beginning to have an odd effect on her. She had an actress friend who had always sworn that once in costume, she seemed to live

9

the character she was playing. Lory now found that she knew exactly what Katy meant.

Introductions were performed, and Lory shook hands with the other two women and their male companions, and tried hard to remember their names—but without much success, for the one thought uppermost in her mind was: If this isn't old Mackinnon—if it's the nephew, what will he be like? There was just time to ask, if she was quick.

'You say Mr. Mackinnon is young? Is it his guest-house?'

'Oh yes,' answered Edna. 'The old laird died two or three years ago, and Grant took over the place—and the island too,' and she smiled at her twin, as if at some secret known only to the two of them. Lory found her heart beating faster as she watched the Range-Rover draw to a halt a few yards away. This was a different proposition altogether. But the question was: was it for better or for worse?

And then he was coming towards them, and her heart skipped a beat, and her first absurd thought was—oh dear! I hope he's not like his great-uncle! For if he was, what a formidable opponent. He was like one of those giants you glimpsed occasionally on television when they showed excerpts from the Highland Games. The only thing he needed to complete the picture was a pair of bagpipes—or alternatively, a caber, and he looked as though he would have no difficulty in tossing one a record distance. Black hair, broad shoulders, a seaman's jersey—and a rather tattered-looking kilt which nevertheless looked entirely right on him. And he swung towards them and proceeded to shake hands with everyone, leaving Lory, who now stood slightly at the back, to the last.

He was even more formidable at close quarters—for anyone with a faintly guilty conscience, that is, and Lory's was doing little flips of apprehension—and his handshake was as solid as the rest of him, and she hid a wince as he said, in a pleasantly deep voice: 'Mackinnon. You'll be Miss Stevenson?'

'Yes. How d'you do?'

His eyes were dark blue, the colour of the sea in the morning, and his face was strong and firm, with a wide mouth and stubborn chin, and his neck was as thick as a footballer's, and his nose had a faintly crooked look to it as if he'd broken it at some time and never bothered to do anything about it. Those eyes were on her now, but not with any spark of interest, for which she felt an odd mixture of emotions—annoyance and relief combined.

'Welcome to Creagdubh——' He would be more at home speaking the Gaelic. There was that lilt to his voice, oddly at variance with his appearance, that told her of his origins. Here was a true, dyed-in-the-wool Hebridean. 'I hope you will enjoy your stay with us.'

'Thank you.' She smiled and had to push the granny glasses up her nose, for they had the disconcerting habit of slipping.

'We'll away now. Aye well, Dougall. You've unloaded the supplies, I see. I'll return for them when I come back for the luggage.' He left Lory and strode over to bid his farewells to the pilot, a big man himself, who was dwarfed by Grant Mackinnon. Lory followed her new companions towards the waiting Range-Rover, and looked back to see the two men heaving cases and boxes to one side of the runway, presumably to be out of the way of the plane as it taxied off.

Well, that's it, thought Lory, listening with only one ear to the chatter of the two women who had clearly decided to take her under their wing. Now I've met him, I know the worst. All the stories her father had told her about old Mackinnon faded before the reality of this man, the laird of Creagdubh. This was the one she had to deceive.

If Lory's first surprise had been her host, her second came at the sight of the big house where she was due to stay for the next three weeks. Of solid granite, it stood proudly on a hill overlooking the large island, a vast sprawling grey mansion with a huge walled garden, and greenhouses, and outbuildings, and a certain wildness to the grounds that stirred Lory's heart. It was as if the place itself was entirely in keeping with its surroundings, as if it would withstand storm and tempest, and defy them all for ever. Creagdubh House! It should have been Creagdubh Castle.

Edna touched her arm and pointed out of the window of the Range-Rover to where several sheep and goats grazed on the grass near the drive. 'This is what it's like,' she whispered, although it was doubtful if their driver would hear above the drumming of the engine as it throbbed upwards ever nearer the house. 'And when you get inside, you'll know why we come back each year.'

Lory smiled and nodded, but her thoughts were different. So Grant Mackinnon lived in comfort, did he? Did the islanders appreciate that, she wondered, did they accept it as his due, while they existed under primitive conditions in their tiny crofts from where they scraped a living from the soil? She felt her hand tighten instinctively on the briefcase set securely on her knee. It was all inside there, all the information she had gathered painstakingly from various sources over the past months. In the privacy of her room she would study it again, and tomorrow she would begin her task. She looked at Grant Mackinnon in the driving seat. He didn't look a monster, but there was a certain set to his shoulders that told of determination. He would be a hard man to cross. Perhaps they were frightened of him. He had appeared pleasant enough to the little group from the plane—but he was making money from them, wasn't he? That was the difference. Lory bit her lip. She hated injustice of any kind. But at the same time, she must reserve judgement until she had spoken to various islanders. For what if Grant Mackinnon was much different from his great-uncle? He might be doing his best to help them. She would soon see. A small niggling doubt at the back of her mind refused to go away. He had been there how long, two years? Time enough to have begun—and yet the most

12

recent report she had in her briefcase—from the previous nurse, who had left the island only six months previously— gave no indication that anything had improved.

'I'm sorry?' She was startled back to the present by Edna's voice in her ear.

'We're here!'

She was holding everyone up. Confused, Lory scrambled along the seat, and crouching, jumped on to the rough gravel of the drive, helped by the strong hand of Grant Mackinnon, who gave her the briefest of glances before assisting Edna and Joan from the vehicle.

The two couples were already on their way up the stone steps. Lory looked up at the blank sky-reflecting windows at each side and above the giant pillared entrance way. There was a certain bleakness about the place now that she was near. And that too was in keeping, for was not Creag-dubh itself a bleak island? Outermost of the Hebrides, swept by the cruel Atlantic winds and tides, it could be nothing else. Here were no tall graceful trees, only bushes and shrubs, sturdy enough to withstand anything. She would be interested to see his vegetable garden, although she guessed that the walls of the garden had been built for just such a purpose. The outbuildings were hidden from view now. There would be time to explore later, when she had settled in and locked her briefcase safely away.

He was behind her as she followed the two women into the hall, and for a moment his hand brushed hers as he held the door open. The hall was wide, with a fireplace, and in it a log fire set, but unlit. The walls were dark oak-panelled, making it almost gloomy, but yet at the same time beautiful.

'I'll call Elspeth to show you all to your rooms,' Grant Mackinnon said. 'And then I dare say she'll have had the kettle on for a cup of tea.' And he smiled at them all. The smile transformed his face, crinkling his eyes, showing his strong white teeth, softening the hard planes of cheeks and stubborn chin.

Why, thought Lory, he's an attractive man—and fought the momentary weakness away. He could be her enemy, that was what she had to remember.

'And then I'll away back for your luggage.' He strode towards a darkly shadowed corridor and bellowed: 'Elspeth, *b'idh mi falbh!*'

'Aye, well, off you go, then,' a distant voice answered, in English, and then faint footsteps sounded, coming nearer, and a woman appeared. At first she was just a shadow in a doorway, and then she stepped into the hall and smiled at them all. The high clear voice had sounded as if it might come from a young woman, but Elspeth was well past middle age, with white fluffy hair and rosy cheeks—and a smile of such utter radiance that Lory felt instinctively drawn towards her.

She greeted them all by name, shook hands with Lory, said briskly to Grant: 'Do not be long now, the dinner will be ready soon, and I'll give these good people their *strupach* after they've seen their rooms.' He waved, and strode out of the door, and as Lory and the others climbed the stairs, she heard the roar of the Range-Rover, and the scattering of gravel as he turned it round. Then the noise died away. Something had gone with his leaving. Like him or not, Lory knew instinctively that he was a man not to be ignored. He—it was ridiculous, she told herself, but it was as if he vibrated a kind of strength and power. Yet he seemed softly spoken and well mannered, not brash or brusque.

She was the last to reach her room, and was glad of the fact, for Elspeth went into the bedroom with her, and crossed to the window.

'See,' she said, 'we have given you this as you are come here for the first time.'

Lory, curious, followed the housekeeper, looked out and gasped in pleasure. Below her was the kitchen garden, securely walled—and beyond it, black rocks and cliffs—and a sheer drop to the sea. And beyond that, there was nothing. The sea stretched away, smooth and almost golden in the early evening sunlight to the distant horizon.

She took a deep breath. 'How beautiful,' she murmured, shaken.

'Aye, it is.' Elspeth turned round and surveyed Lory with bright blue eyes that were as young as a girl's. 'There's nothing beyond there until you reach America.'

This was an opportunity. 'This island is very remote, isn't it?' she asked. 'Nearly as far out as St. Kilda, in fact.'

Elspeth looked at her oddly. 'That's a fact,' she agreed, mildly enough. 'But the difference is, this island is still inhabited. They took everyone away from St. Kilda in 1930—and whether they were right or wrong, it is not for me to say. Look you now, see the vegetables growing down below. They are Mackinnon's pride and joy.' It had been a deliberate change of subject, Lory knew, and wondered if any faint rumours had preceded her. But how could anyone know? It was her over-sensitive imagination at work.

'Yes, I can see,' she agreed. 'Is it possible to walk round there?'

'Och yes. Mackinnon'll no mind.'

'You must keep busy here,' said Lory pleasantly, keeping on safe ground.

'We are, but only in summer. No one will venture here in winter, of course—and why should they? It is far too rough for gently bred folks.' She patted Lory's arm. 'There now, I'm talking too much. I'll away and pour out the tea. Come down as soon as you like. The big lounge just the other side of the hall it is. And you'll meet a few of the others.'

She bustled out and Lory stared after her thoughtfully. That gentle face was slightly deceptive. Behind it, she sensed that Elspeth possessed a shrewd brain, and more, was devoted to Mackinnon, as she referred to him. And to the island.

She went over to the washbasin in a corner of the large airy room and rinsed her face and hands. There was one advantage about wearing no cosmetics—no touching up was necessary after a wash. She adjusted the spectacles, frowned at her reflection in the mirror, and went out and down the stairs.

Even had she not known where the main lounge was, she would have found it by the noise. For some reason she had supposed there would only be seven guests at Creagdubh House, and she stopped in astonishment as she reached the door, and hesitated. There were at least fifteen people sitting round in comfortable-looking red armchairs, and she could see among them Edna and Joan, talking to two men—not the ones who had travelled on the plane—and Edna looked up and waved.

'Here we are, dear. Come and meet our friends.'

It was again most odd. Usually when Lory entered a room full of people, heads turned, male heads that is, and she was used to it, expected—and enjoyed it. Now, an inexplicable sensation of shyness smote her as she walked across, and although most heads had turned at Edna's call, it was merely out of curiosity, and she was greeted with smiles and encouraging little nods—as though she really was a timid little thing who could do with kind words to help her on her way.

Heavens! she thought, what shall I do? This is terrible. If I'm not careful I'll be blushing soon, and that's something I haven't done since I was about twelve!

She sank into the spare armchair with gratitude. At least no one was looking now. The two men sitting with Edna and Joan rose politely as they were introduced, and Lory thought: they're rather nice. Two more contrasting types could hardly be imagined. Raymond Bell was a small man with white moustache and lovely shining bald head, and twinkling brown eyes. Ellis Hawkins should have been a pirate with that fierce red beard—but his manner was kind, and he seemed even a little shy. All were old acquaintants, that was clear, and drew Lory into their circle with great ease. Joan poured out a cup of tea and handed it to Lory. Over the chink of teacups, the talk proceeded, and she

16

listened politely, and nodded in all the right places, and hoped that they wouldn't fire too many questions at her. And then she heard it distantly—the arrival of the Range-Rover, and her heart gave a little lurch.

He was back with their luggage. She heard a door slam, then the front door open, and the clatter of the boots he wore on the stone steps—and so engrossed was she in listening that she failed to realize that the others were actually talking about him until Joan said: 'Do you think so, Lory? We may call you Lory, may we?'

'Oh yes, of course. Please do. I'm sorry, what was it you said?'

'About Grant Mackinnon. What's your first impression of him?'

'Oh!' And how could she answer that? 'He seems very well organized, and quite—er—quite young.' Had she said the right thing? And why should she feel so confused about a perfectly simple question? She took refuge in her tea cup.

'I'd say early thirties, wouldn't you, Ellis?' said Joan, her round face beaming at her red-bearded companion.

He was a man of few words. 'Oh—yes, about that,' he agreed.

Edna sighed. 'He's a strange man, though. Oh, I don't mean anything *wrong*. He's always been perfectly pleasant to Joan and me, hasn't he, love? But—well, he seems a real loner to me, the kind of man who's very self-sufficient, and doesn't need people. Elspeth is a gem. How he'd manage this place without her, I don't know——'

And then Lory, horrified, realized that the footsteps were now running up the stairs in the house itself, which could only mean that Grant Mackinnon was carrying everyone's luggage up to their bedrooms—and she had left her brief-case on her bed! She had had it open during the plane flight, and couldn't remember if she had locked it. And if—*if*—he looked inside, her visit would be over before it began.

She stood up hastily. 'Excuse me——' she began, 'I must just——'

'Are you all right, dear?' said Edna anxiously.

'Oh yes—but I've just remembered, I had a wash before I came down, and I think I left my tap on. If Mr. Mackinnon's taking the cases up and sees, I'd hate him to think I was a careless guest.' Even to herself, it sounded feeble, but it was the best she could do on the spur of the moment, and the others nodded sympathetically, as if it was the most natural thing in the world. Feeling wretched at having to tell so many lies, Lory fled.

She ran up the stairs as if pursued, reached the corridor leading to her room—to see Grant Mackinnon's kilted figure just vanishing inside it.

CHAPTER TWO ·

RELIEF washed over Lory. Followed by dismay. How did you explain following your host about? She went into the room to see him putting her case down by the window. He turned as he heard her, and straightened up slowly.

'Oh, hello,' she said. 'I'm glad I've caught you. I'd like to pay you now, in advance, if I may.' It was what she had intended all along anyway, and there was hardly a better time.

He frowned. 'It's not necessary,' he said slowly. 'We don't expect our guests to leave without paying.' He nodded towards the window. 'There is not far you can go anyway.' His eyes were cool on her.

Lory gave a little laugh to show she appreciated his joke. 'No, I dare say not, unless you're a good swimmer, of course. But I've got the cash, and—well, I'm a little scatterbrained about money. I'd feel happier if you took it.' She spared a glance at the bed. Her briefcase lay there quite innocently.

'As you wish,' he shrugged. 'If you would care to give it me now, I will prepare a receipt for you.'

'Oh, thank you.' She fumbled in her bag as if searching, although she knew exactly where her wallet was, but it gave her a moment's respite. And as she looked down, busily engaged, her glasses fell off.

'Damn!' the exclamation came out before she could stop it, and as she instinctively grabbed for them, she dropped her bag—and its contents were strewn on the carpet. In dismayed horror, she knelt down—as did Grant Mackin-

19

non, at the same moment. Was there anything in her hand-bag to give her away? That was the question uppermost in her mind as she scooped frantically for the tissues, lipsticks, perfume, purse, make-up, wallet—oh, why did she have to carry such an enormous bag with her?

Patiently he handed her the more scattered objects, his face an impassive mask, as if pretending not to actually know that anything was amiss. He handed her a small bottle of perfume, expressionless. Would he wonder what she was doing with one of the world's expensive scents in her bag? Or would he, as she hoped, know nothing about such things? She could hardly ask him.

'Thank you. Oh dear, I'm so clumsy!'

'Accidents will happen,' he said, but was there puzzle-ment in his voice? Everything was safely gathered, they both stood up, and Lory put her bag on the bed and opened her wallet.

'I'll put everything straight later,' she said. 'Now, the money. Here you are. That is right, isn't it?'

He took the notes and counted them. 'Yes. Thank you, Miss Stevenson. I'll away now——' he stopped, his eye apparently caught by something behind her. 'Don't move. Your glasses are on the carpet by your feet.' He stooped and picked them up, but even as she reached to take them from him he held them up to the light. 'No, they are not damaged, fortunately. Will I adjust the ear-pieces for you?'

In a second he would discover something that she didn't really want him—or anyone else, for that matter—to know. That the lenses were of plain glass.

'Oh no, really—please—I—it doesn't matter——'

'Ach, it is no trouble. You can manage without them for a few minutes, can you? Then I will return them. It is just a matter of curving this ear-piece a little more——' he held them in his big strong hands, and traced along with his right forefinger. 'See? Do you see?'

'Oh—yes—thank you, but it's all right, *really*. I c-can do it——' to her horror Lory was beginning to stammer. And she reached out to take them, willing him silently to hand them to her. And he did so. For a moment their eyes met across the few feet separating them, and there was something in his gaze that she found immensely disturbing. His was a glance possessing an infinite shrewdness, a depth that she had rarely seen in anyone before, and while under normal circumstances she would not have cared, just then, at that moment, she felt exposed and vulnerable, like some creature under a microscope.

Lory turned away. 'Thank you for your help,' she said. 'How long will dinner be?'

'About thirty minutes.' He was walking towards the door as he answered. 'The dining room is through the lounge. I think you will find it without any trouble. I will away now and unload the rest of the provisions.' And with that he was gone.

Lory sat down on the bed and looked at the glasses. She wished she had never bothered to wear them now. In fact the whole situation was beginning to assume an air of shabby deceit. She put her hand to her chin. Why hadn't she come openly, told him that she was doing a survey—that she was a sociologist employed by the government—and that her priorities in work were investigating living standards on his kind of island with a view to either trying to improve the situation—or when all else failed, trying to persuade the people to leave and establish homes for themselves on the mainland?

She sighed. She knew the answers in advance. Because he would tell her she was an interfering busybody, that he was quite capable of deciding the rights and wrongs—she knew all the answers he would give, for it had happened before, although not to her personally, but to colleagues, also sociologists who had done similar field work on similar remote islands and communities. And she had come here as the result of a personal challenge. Her father had known Grant Mackinnon's great-uncle. They had had a brief bitter clash years previously when John Stevenson, then a young

21

man, had been involved in a legal wrangle with the then middle-aged Ruari Mackinnon over fishing rights on a remote stretch of river in Ross-shire. Her father had won, but the fight had not been forgotten, and when he had heard that someone was needed to go to Creagdubh, after a rather disturbing report from the newly left district nurse, he had pulled a few strings to enable Lory to go. A man of humour, he thought it would be an interesting experience for her, and as he was a senior civil servant himself, the job had not been too difficult to arrange. He was a great cutter of red tape.

Lory sighed again. She could do with him here now. And then she dismissed the thought. What are you, she asked herself sternly, a woman or a mouse? You're twenty-three—almost twenty-four, and you're perfectly capable of dealing with any situation, and you're not doing anything criminal or dishonest, you are merely doing your *job*. And she gave a brisk nod that nearly caused her glasses to fly off again. 'Damn the things!' she muttered, but her confidence and natural good humour were fully restored. She stood up and set about unpacking her suitcase.

Fifteen minutes later, with the briefcase safely hidden away at the bottom of the huge wardrobe, Lory went downstairs to dinner.

It was mid-June, and she knew that the nights were short, but it was still a surprise to find the light still as bright and clear after dinner as it would be mid-morning in London. People drifted away from their tables as they finished eating, and some stopped for a few words at the table Lory and the others occupied, and were introduced to her by Joan and Edna. She was busily engaged in observing her fellow guests, because in her line of work it came as naturally as breathing to do so, and although all were individuals, nevertheless there was a similarity about them, a generally pleasant easy-going air, and she wondered if all bird-watchers were the same. Some day there would be material for a book in that, she thought—musing over a title . . .

'Did you like the food?' Joan interrupted her thoughts.

'Mm? Oh yes! Lovely.' Lory surveyed the empty plates before them. 'And I was starving too,' she confessed.

Edna laughed. 'It's the air, dear, that's the way it gets you. We always have to go on a diet when we get home, don't we, Joan?' And they both laughed heartily at the thought.

The two men had moved away, and Lory sensed that they were impatient to be out and away—and it didn't take a mathematical genius to sense that while four might be company, five was not. She smiled at her two kindly companions. 'Will you excuse me?' she asked them. 'I'm going up to my room to finish unpacking'—how easily the fibs came! 'And then I'd like a little walk.'

'Oh, but——' Edna looked slightly flustered, a mingling of relief and concern, 'wouldn't you like to come for a walk with us? You'd be very welcome.'

'Thank you, I know I would, but I'm sure you've got lots to talk about, and you've already looked after me so well, I feel quite at home now.' She stood up, to settle the matter. 'Did you say that coffee was served in the lounge after ten? Perhaps I'll see you then.' And she smiled brightly at them both, and with a little wave of the hand, went quickly out of the dining room.

Safely up in her room, she stood by the window and looked out over the sea, so deceptively calm-looking from a distance, glittering in the late evening sunlight, and her heart ached at the sheer beauty of it all, of the black rocks below, the white spray constantly dashing against them. On an impulse she opened her window wide and took in deep breaths of salty air. She could hear the faint roar now, the roar and thunder of the waves hurling themselves in constant battle with the rocks. The black rocks of Creagdubh. And nearer to, the outbuildings, greenhouses, long wall, plants and vegetables growing in defiance of the elements.

23

Lory sighed. She could understand anybody loving it here. And Grant Mackinnon fitted into the place as naturally as the rocks did. She was going to have to be very careful. Very careful indeed.

She looked at her watch. Nearly ten, and her father would be waiting for her call. Edna had told her at dinner that there was a telephone box at the far end of the village—the only telephone on the entire island. And what was more natural than to walk down there? Lory went to her wardrobe and took out her short black jacket. One last quick look in the mirror—although she was beginning to wonder why; it was hardly necessary, she always looked the *same* now—and she was ready to go.

She set off briskly from the house, in case anyone was watching—after all, bird-watchers would really *enjoy* walking, wouldn't they? She was thankful now for the sensible flat shoes she wore, and the air was so bright and clear that it began to be an actual pleasure after the first few minutes of realizing that for the next three whole weeks, anywhere she wanted to go would have to be reached on foot, for she could hardly see Grant Mackinnon lending her his Range-Rover—especially if he knew for what reason.

Lory's high spirits began to assert themselves before she had even reached the end of the drive. 'Study in Human Adaptability,' she thought aloud. Hmm, that would make a good title for an article on how easy—or difficult—it was for human beings to adapt themselves to a changed environment. She remembered a series in a newspaper, not long previously, in which a reporter had been deliberately left on a deserted Hebridean island for two weeks with a small supply of food—only to be used in *dire* emergency— a distress flare, knives and rope and matches, and waterproof clothing. His daily diary of what had begun as an ordeal had gradually told of his acceptance and adjustment to the toughness of his existence. And the 'after' photos had shown a slimmer, fitter, deeply tanned specimen of manhood. She had kept the articles. And here am I, she thought, wondering if I'll cope, because I've been used to having it easy, and there's no comparison really, I'm sleeping in a comfortable bed, eating excellent food—if that first meal is anything to go by—and I've got people to talk to as well. Plus a job to do. And Lory laughed out loud at the sheer joy of it all, and a pair of seagulls wheeling overhead cried out harshly in reply.

There was no one within sight. She walked a narrow rutted road, and on both sides of her the rugged hills, rock-strewn, covered in scrubby grass and heather and bushes, stretched away seemingly endlessly. It was a three-mile walk to the village, and for Lory, just at that moment, she could have been completely alone in this strange, beautiful world of dark greens and greys. The silence was profound and overwhelming, and the only signs of movement were when what she had thought to be a distant rock stirred, and she saw that it was a sheep.

Where were all the other guests? Could over a dozen people vanish completely? It seemed they had. But the island was large, and there would be no reason for anyone to go down to the village when no shops would be open. Lory had memorized a map of Creagdubh, and she knew that nearer to the house, in the opposite direction, there were cliffs and rocks where various birds nested. There was also a small track down to the shore, and many other paths. There was really nothing to interest ornithologists on the side of the island to which she was going. That was a good thing. There would be nobody to see her when she began talking to the villagers. But perhaps there was only one person who really counted, and who could tell, with him? No use in speculation, Lory told herself, just take each day as it comes, and see what happens. And squaring her shoulders, she began to walk more briskly.

A sleepy and surprised-sounding operator answered after Lory had dinged the buttons of the telephone up and down a few times.

'I'd like to make a call to London,' she said. She hadn't really expected the phone to be on S.T.D., but it meant that both she and her father would have to be careful what they said. She gave the woman the number and waited through an interminable number of clicks and buzzes until she heard a familiar voice. Feeding the ten-pence pieces in hastily, she said: 'Hello. Father?'

'Hello, love. No pips?'

'No. We're not on S.T.D.'

'Ah!' It was a long-drawn-out, meaningful 'ah'. They had already discussed the possibility of this happening, and there was no fear of her father saying anything indiscreet. 'And how are you settling in? Everything all right?'

'Oh yes, Creagdubh House is lovely, and it's run by a Mr. Mackinnon—I believe he took over from his great-uncle who died a couple of years ago.'

'Ah!' An even longer, more meaningful sound. 'I *see*. And have you had a chance to look round the island yet?'

'I've just come through the village to get to the telephone. Some nice little cottages, and a shop. There are *dozens* of varieties of birds living here——' she injected a note of enthusiasm in her voice for the benefit of anyone who might be eavesdropping. 'I'm sure I'm going to have a very interesting holiday.'

'That's good, dear. Well, write to me when you can, won't you?'

'I will, Daddy, as soon as I get time. I'll go now—I've got a three-mile walk back—still, you know me. I *love* walking.' She knew he would appreciate the humour of that, and his muffled snort of laughter told her he had. They said their goodbyes, and Lory left the telephone box.

A wind had sprung up, and although she had become almost used to the constant breeze, this was stronger, less teasing, colder. She shivered and pushed her hands deeper into her pockets. Smoke whirled away from the chimney of one of the cottages, and a window was lighted, but the rest were silent as if people were in bed. And so she was able, now that the telephone call was behind her, to look more closely at the houses of the village. Perhaps the softening evening light helped, but they did not seem as bleak as they had first appeared to her on her way along before. They were all uniformly small, square, some with thatched and some with corrugated iron roofs. There was no road, as such, just a wide track along which Lory was picking her way carefully.

The whole atmosphere was vaguely and disturbingly depressing. And now that she had seen the place, she couldn't wait to get back to her notes, and read them in the light of her new knowledge. The loch lay behind the row of houses on her right, the water grim and forbidding because the sun had vanished behind a cloud, and two or three fishing boats swayed and creaked gently by the shore. What a contrast here from Creagdubh House! How very different it was. How desolate the hills rising from the other side of the loch so barren and exposed to the elements. Lory could imagine what it would be like in winter, and an unaccustomed sense of depression came over her. She must try and help, she knew that now, more certainly than she had before.

Plunging her hands deeper still in her pockets, Lory began to stride it out back to Creagdubh House. And then, even as she left the straggle of houses, she saw her first islander. There was a larger building set back from the road, clearly a schoolhouse, with cottage attached, and the long thin path led down to a wooden gate with semi-circular wooden arch. And on the gate a middle-aged man was leaning, puffing contentedly at a pipe.

'Good evening,' he called.

Lory slowed her steps. 'Good evening,' she answered, smiling. Her first interview, if she played her cards right; and handed to her on a plate, metaphorically speaking. 'Is this the school?'

'Aye, that it is. You'll—eh—be a visitor, then?'

They were now standing facing each other across the

closed gate. 'Yes, I'm staying at Creagdubh House. I've just been to telephone home, let them know I'm here safely.'

'Aye, I was watching you from the window, and I said to my wife, she'll be away to the telephone box, and so you were.' He nodded in a satisfied manner, a pleasant ruddy-cheeked man with a small bristly moustache. 'And now you're away back home to Creagdubh. Ach, it's daft, them not having a telephone, but there, old Mackinnon wouldn'a touch the things, and young Mackinnon is of a like mind, I'm thinking.'

She had to be careful. 'Where I come from, the telephone can be a mixed blessing. Perhaps he likes the old ways better, who knows? I mean, maybe too many modern things here would spoil the atmosphere.' And she smiled warmly, and waited.

He snorted. 'He'd have one put in if it suited him. But I'm no mind-reader—and who can tell what that young fellow is thinking anyway? He's a dark one, he is——'

'The house is very comfortable, though,' Lory put in, as if fearing that he might think she was criticizing. 'I'm sure he's a very good host.'

'Ach, I'm sure he is. Though I wouldn't know, never having stayed there myself, and only been there once or twice. The old laird didn't encourage callers——' and then he stopped, as if he might have said too much.

'Oh!' Lory's surprise was genuine. 'But I thought it had been a guest-house for several years?'

'Oh aye, but he left Elspeth to look after the visitors, and he kept well out of the way. She's a saint, that woman is. How she put up with his ways no one can understand, but there, women are funny creatures,' and he grinned amiably as if to make sure Lory wouldn't take offence, something she had absolutely no intention of doing.

She laughed. 'He sounds as if he was quite a character.'

'You could put it that way. Young Grant's better, if that means anything,' and he sniffed.

'Oh, I'm sure he is,' she said, earnestly, and blinked behind the granny glasses. She found herself slipping into the rôle with more ease each time she spoke to anyone. Heavens, she thought, I hope the change isn't permanent! And she decided to do something about it the minute she got back to Creagdubh House. 'Tell me,' she went on, 'for coming from London as I do, I find islands like this *so* interesting. Does Mr. Mackinnon *own* all the houses on it, or do they belong to the islanders themselves?'

'Och, they're all his. Except this schoolhouse we live in. That's government property, so he has nothing to do with it. Come away in and look round—we're all modern. We have the electricity too!' he added proudly.

'Heavens! I'd love to, but I'm sure your wife won't appreciate visitors at this time of night, Mr.——?'

'Macleod, Donald Macleod. Ach, she'll not mind. She's the schoolteacher, you see. You'll have a cup of tea and then be on your way.' And he opened the gate.

A few minutes later Lory was inside the extremely warm and comfortable living room of the schoolhouse. Mrs. Macleod, a placid plump woman who sat knitting, looked up over her horn-rimmed glasses at Lory and smiled. 'Well, this is a pleasure, Donald,' she said in a soft Highland lilt. 'Do you go and get the cups. Sit down, my dear.' She pointed to the chair opposite her on which a huge tabby cat lay curled fast asleep. 'Just push the cat off, he'll not mind. He should not be there anyway. Unless you don't like the cats, that is?' she frowned anxiously.

'I love them,' Lory assured her. 'It seems such a shame to disturb him, though,' and she picked up the enormous creature which immediately started to purr like a fire engine and nestle into her coat.

'There now, he's taken to you!' said Mrs. Macleod in surprise. 'Would you look at this, Donald,' she called towards the kitchen from where a clatter of crockery told that Mr. Macleod was doing his bit as host.

The cat curled up on Lory's knee, and stroking it, she

said: 'I hope I'm not disturbing her. I know it's late, but Mr. Macleod asked me——'

'Hush! You're most welcome. It's not often we get visitors at all. You'll be staying at the Big House, then?'

'Yes. And my name's Lory Stevenson. I'd just been to phone my father and was on my way back there.'

'Aye, we saw you going. A good night for a walk, is it not?'

'Oh yes, and the air's so fresh here. I'm sure I'll sleep like a log tonight.'

'That you will. Ah, here's the man himself. Do you have sugar, Miss Stevenson?'

'Call me Lory, please. No sugar, thanks.'

Mr. Macleod pulled up a stool and sat down, balancing his cup and saucer uneasily as if he would prefer to be holding a pint glass. 'I was just telling Mi—Lory about young Mackinnon,' he began.

'Tsk! I hope you've not been gossiping again, Donald!' his wife chided with a smile at Lory.

'No, we were talking generally. But I asked her in to see round, that's all.'

'Bragging about the electric, no doubt! I know you of old.'

He winked sheepishly at Lory, who saw an opportunity. 'But don't they all have electricity here?' she asked.

The couple looked at one another as if Lory had asked whether Martians dwelt on Creagdubh. It was Mrs. Macleod who answered. 'Apart from the Big House itself, we are the only ones on the island who have it,' she said, then seeing Lory's astonishment—which she tried hard to hide, but apparently without success: 'It costs money, you see. We have our own dynamo, run from the mountain streams above the house. And I dare say it could be done elsewhere, but——' she shrugged, her plump face warm with concern, 'what can one do?'

'It seems awful,' Lory whispered. Yet she knew she should not have been so surprised. Was it not all part of the pattern? 'But the villagers—don't they mind?'

'Ach, they have never known differently, have they? To them, the "electric" is some new-fangled invention of the devil. They are a very God-fearing crowd here.'

'And no doubt Mr. Mackinnon encourages that attitude,' murmured Lory softly, scarcely aware that she spoke aloud, until Donald Macleod answered her.

'Aye, well, you could be right. But I dare say it's not for us to judge.'

'Do you have a doctor on Creagdubh?' Lory enquired, knowing the answer full well, but hoping it would lead on to other things . . .

'A doctor? No. There is the nurse, though, and a very capable body she is too, as good as a doctor any day, I'd say,' Mrs. Macleod answered. 'Wouldn't you think, Donald?'

'Oh aye, she is that.'

'And I suppose she's been here a while?' murmured Lory.

'Ach, five minutes, it seems like. You'll no doubt meet her if you come down here again, she's just next door.' And then, at Lory's puzzlement, she laughed. 'When I say next door I mean she's away down the road a wee bit, on your way back to Creagdubh House. Just a minute or two from here it is, a nice little house and garden. No, she's fairly new, but—well, she has settled in—better than the last one,' and she gave her husband a brief glance, and then, as if to change the subject, 'Will you have a shortbread with your tea?'

'No, thanks. I must be going now.' Lory looked at her watch. She was consumed with curiosity by the rather odd remark of Mrs. Macleod's—and by the way it had been said. But her instinct told her not to ask further. Not now. There would be time for that later.

The subject changed, they spoke generally about the island for a few more minutes, and then the couple accompanied her to the gate. The wind had dropped, leaving a

31

faint sweet mistiness to the air, and high in the still light sky, a hazy moon.

'You'll have a pleasant walk back, then, and watch out for the Moon-dancers,' said Mr. Macleod. 'That's supposed to be lucky, although it is only at the full moon, they say.'

This was something new to Lory. 'The Moon-dancers?' she repeated. 'What a lovely word. But what does it mean?'

'Has no one told you yet?' Mr. Macleod looked faintly surprised. 'Our very own legend as well!'

'You can't expect everyone to be interested in these old tales, Donald,' answered Mrs. Macleod. She spoke to Lory kindly. ''Tis just some old Celtic folklore, about the Little People—the fairies, you'd call them, and how they'll dance at midnight when there's a full moon if ever anything important is about to happen. Now I'm a teacher, and I deal in facts, not old superstitions, but—well——' she shrugged her plump shoulders, 'I'll never scoff at certain things, even though I *know* there's no such things as fairies.' She gave a little laugh. 'There now, don't look so scared, dear. You won't see them tonight anyway. The moon is too new.'

Sudden fascination gripped Lory. She knew it was *absurd* to be so interested, but at the same time, a little frisson of excitement ran up her spine. 'But where are they—I mean, where does *legend* say they are seen?' she asked.

'Why, near the Big House itself, on the sea, where else?' answered Mrs. Macleod. 'I'll tell you what, I have a little book somewhere which mentions the tale. I'll look it out for you. Call in next time you are passing, and you may borrow it.'

'Oh, yes, thank you. And thanks for the tea. I've really enjoyed my visit.' They said goodbye, and Lory set off down the road home. It wasn't until she turned to give one last wave at the now faintly misty figures by the gate that she realized she hadn't seen over the house after all. She smiled to herself. Next time. She had a lot to think about now, a great deal. The sooner she began making her notes, the better. As soon as she got back in fact.

And then, after she had passed the nurse's house—which was in darkness—and was on the lonely stretch of road which continued for almost three miles, she remembered Mr. Macleod's words: 'Watch out for the Moon-dancers,' and she suddenly wished that he hadn't told her. Not to-night anyway. For there was this utterly lost lonely feeling suddenly, and she could hardly run back to the schoolhouse and tell them she was frightened, and in any case, she was very calm and level-headed, she *knew* she was, so why was there this prickling sensation at the back of her neck, and why did the hills on either side of her seem to *loom* so darkly and almost seem to be—no, of course they weren't moving, it was just the shadows. The shadows on the hills were moving, the bushes and shrubs——

Lory blinked hard and averted her eyes and looked straight ahead at the long and winding, the *never-ending* road that lay in front of her, and she wished for someone, *anyone* to be there with her. Now, she thought, if I walk quickly and count the steps I take, I wonder how many it will be before I get back? Well, allowing for, say, three thousand steps a mile, that will be—er—let me see—it was no use. Her eyes were being drawn irresistibly to one side, up the steep, rough, rocky slope to her right, and to the shape which seemed to be—no, which *was* moving, right at the top. In fascinated horror she watched, even as she walked, trying not to break into a run, and the slight mistiness cleared, and the moving shadow turned into a sheep which suddenly let out a faint long-drawn-out 'baa-aa-aa.'

Her heart was pounding, and now that she had stopped holding her breath she could feel her heart beating in her throat, in her ears, a rushing, pounding sound filling her head and body . . . 'I'll be a nervous wreck before I get back,' she said firmly out loud, and that helped, as did the mental picture of herself staggering up the stone steps at

Creagdubh House, white-haired and trembling and gibbering incoherently. Lory laughed softly, normality restored—or nearly, and then she began walking just a bit more quickly, and counting the steps, concentrating only on that, and putting all other thoughts out of her mind, even the reason for her being there ...

And then she was drowned in white light, and stood transfixed in the middle of the road as a huge nameless beast roared up to devour her. And the Range-Rover halted a few feet before her, and Grant Mackinnon slammed his door and walked towards her.

'So you are here,' he said, and even though she could hardly see him in the lights from the vehicle, and he was just a huge black shape, she had never felt so relieved in all her life to see another human being.

'Yes. Were you—were you looking for *me*?' she gasped.

'Aye. They were worried about you. Your friends at the house.'

'Oh!' Joan and Edna. *Dear* Joan and Edna. She had forgotten all about her promise to see them in the lounge.

'They thought maybe you'd got lost. Come away now, we'll go back.' And he turned and strode to the Range-Rover, leaving Lory to follow. Which she did with alacrity. For there was that uneasy feeling that he might just go without her—which was ridiculous, of course, for hadn't he come to meet her specially? And his manner wasn't annoyed, or anything remotely resembling it. But still ...

Lory slammed her door and settled back into her seat. 'Oh, thank you,' she said. She felt only relief. There was no sense of danger, none at all.

CHAPTER THREE

IT was only when he stopped the Range-Rover that Lory felt the first faint twinge of unease. For they were not within sight of the house, or of anything else in fact, save the bleak towering hills around, and the narrow twisting ribbon of road ahead. And the faintest of mists wreathed round the vehicle, damp, ghostlike.

'Why have we stopped?' she said.

Grant Mackinnon turned very slowly toward her. 'Well,' he answered, in such a pleasant easy tone that she felt herself relaxing, 'this is your first visit to the island, is it not? I was just wondering to myself what your interests were, Miss Stevenson. It is difficult to talk in the house—there is so much to do, as you can imagine, and I wondered if there was perhaps any part of the island you would like to see before we go back in.'

'You're very kind,' she said faintly. 'Of course, I'm interested in the bird sanctuaries—Creagdubh is famous for its birds, isn't it?—and—well——' she shrugged. 'That's about it, isn't it? *Is* there anything else I should see? Apart from the beautiful scenery, of course.' She laughed softly. 'You've given me a delightful room.'

'Aye. We like to do that, the first time. Afterwards you'll maybe have just a view of the drive—that's if you plan to come again. You're an expert on birds, then?'

'Heavens no, I'm just a beginner——' She shouldn't have let herself be lulled by that deceptively gentle manner. There was more to this than just the good host enquiring after his guest's comfort.

'Is that so? Then maybe I'll be able to help. We have a nice library at the house. The books are all quite old, of course—but then birds don't change, do they?'

'I suppose not. I'd certainly like to look through it. I'm interested in all kinds of books.'

'You are? Ach then, you'll spend some time there, I dare say. You do a lot of reading, is it?'

'Oh yes. Lots,' she agreed. Books were a nice *safe* subject. And it was quite true. Lory loved books of all kinds. 'I've brought a couple with me—a historical romance and a thriller. I never go anywhere without a few books, in case I'm left with nothing to do for an hour or two.'

'That's why you wear glasses—for the reading?'

There was a moment's dreadful silence. He knew. He *knew*. There was no doubt about it. His tone had changed. Gone the gentle solicitousness. His voice was quite calm—but hard, oh, so very hard.

'You mean—these?' Lory took them off.

'Aye, I do that. What would anyone be doing wearing spectacles with plain glass in them, I wonder. It's a thought that has been occupying my mind for quite a time, Miss Stevenson.'

'Really?' Lory rallied her defences. 'I would have thought you'd have far more important things to occupy you—like looking after your guests.'

He turned fully towards her. In the dark confines of the vehicle they were only inches away from each other, and the closeness was disturbing. This big dark kilted stranger was no simple Highlander. There was a shrewdness to his eyes, shadowed as they were, that Lory found most unnerving. Then he slid his arm along the back of her seat, a normal enough gesture, but one which now seemed to take on a sinister significance—almost as if she were a prisoner. She took a deep breath, trying to shake off the absurd fancy.

'Perhaps that is what I am trying to do,' he answered softly. 'Now I've heard of women wearing fancy glasses for decoration—and while it is not my intention to insult you,

36

there is no way, not even by a wild stretch of the imagination, that yours could be ornamental.' And he reached out his right hand and took them from her.

Lory gasped. 'How dare you! Give them back to me at *once*!'

Instead of doing so, he held them up to the misty light from outside. Lory attempted to snatch them from him—a move she instantly regretted, but she was too perturbed to think straight. For they were immediately out of reach, and short of an undignified scuffle—and a vain one at that, she knew—there was nothing she could do.

He laughed softly. 'Come now, and I thought you were a quiet one. There is no need to snatch. Here, you may have your glasses back, of course.' And he handed them to her. It seemed pointless to put them back on. Opening her handbag, Lory put them inside. 'So why do you wear them?' he persisted. 'And why do you carry in your bag some very expensive perfumes and make-up when you have no intention of wearing them?'

'You are insufferably rude,' she snapped. 'It's none of your business.'

'Indeed? You are quite right, of course. What you carry with you *is* none of my affair—but it makes me think, you see, and the more I think about it, the less it adds up. And then I look at your hair, and I see it scraped back into——'

'You've said enough! Now will you——'

'Into a very strange-looking bun,' he went on, as if she hadn't spoken. 'And I say to myself that Miss Lory Stevenson is clearly trying to disguise herself—and why would that be?' And his left hand, the one resting so casually along the back of her seat, went up, and the next moment she felt his fingers pulling at the pins as he said: 'Let us see you as nature intended.'

It was the last straw. Incensed, Lory, spitting fire and fury, was at him. But not for more than a few seconds. The brief, inglorious struggle was over before it had begun, and she faced him, panting and dishevelled, her hair tumbling free, her eyes sparking fire, her cheeks flushed and rosy, her breast heaving. And Grant Mackinnon switched on the interior light and flooded her with yellow warmth.

'Ah,' he said, on a long sigh. 'That is more like it.'

She struck out at him, aiming for his face, catching his cheek in a satisfying resounding slap, about to follow it up with another when he caught and held her flailing hands. 'Do not hit me,' he said. 'I don't like it, and I'm not one of your Sassenach cissies who lets the women boss him around. Just calm down, little wildcat——'

'Let me go at once!' she breathed, struggling.

'When you promise to control yourself.'

Lory stopped struggling. 'That's it,' he said, and let go of her hands. She began to rub the wrists he had held so firmly.

'I could have you up for assault,' she said, 'and how would your guests like that? They'd not be in such a hurry to come again.'

He laughed softly. 'You'll have a long way to go to find a policeman—back to the mainland, in fact. And where are your bruises? You call my defending myself an assault? You are in no danger of being struck by me, I promise you that. But I won't have strangers coming to my house posing as something they are not——'

'Don't be ridiculous! Posing indeed! Do you want to see my cheque book?—you'll find out my name's my own.'

'Yet you prefer to pay cash?'

'So? There's no law about it, is there? Unless *you* make the laws round here.' Her voice was touched with irony.

'Ach no, of course not. But you tried to give me the impression that you were a wee bit—eh—daft with money, which was why you wanted to pay me straight away. Now if that's the case, why carry money around with you at all?'

Lory turned away and looked out of the window at the gathering mist outside. 'I think I'll walk back to the house,' she said. 'I don't intend to sit here all night exchanging insults with you.' She tried to make her voice very casual. He was clever, far too clever.

'Unless,' he went on softly, 'unless you thought that by paying cash *right away*, as soon as you arrived, you would be quite sure that I couldn't ask you to leave.'

It wasn't so much that he was near the point—he was bang on target. In a minute, Lory felt, he would probably tell her who she was, *why* she was there, how much she earned. She didn't want to hear. She grasped the door handle, began to turn it—and he reached over and locked the door.

'No,' he said. 'I wouldn't if I were you.'

'You can't stop me——'

'The track is narrow. I've stopped near a drop. If you step out now you'll as like as not break your ankle.'

'And that would suit you, wouldn't it?' she snapped, fear making her edgy.

'No, we have enough to do without looking after invalids.'

'Then take me back to the house at once. I've had enough of your insults——'

'And I'd hardly begun. Why are you here?' The question was blunt, deliberately so.

Lory turned round, very slowly. The whole situation had begun to assume the proportions of a nightmare. He had this inexorable quality to him—she had the dreadful feeling that he would keep on and on, not letting her go—until she told him. The mist-swathed vehicle only added to the sense of isolation, as if they were the only two people in the world, and there could be no escape from him, none at all. The tension was almost a tangible thing, surrounding them, crackling between them like electricity, overwhelming—disturbing.

'All right,' she said. 'I'll tell you why I'm here. I'm not on holiday, I'm working. And I'm not a bird-watcher, I'm a sociologist. And I've come to make a report about this island and find out if all the things we've heard about it are true—and see what we can do about it——'

'We? Who is "we"?' His voice was harsh.

'My employers—a government department——'

'I need no snoopers here—especially not you——'

'That is precisely why I'm here in "disguise", as you call it. I didn't expect the welcome mat out, believe me—but I'm here to help you, in actual fact, whether you care to believe it or not——'

'I don't! Help us! *Dia*, we would need help with people like you here, interfering. What do you know about life on an island? You with your city clothes and ways—and cars everywhere—the soft life, that's what you're used to—ach, don't talk to me!' The Macleods, on her visit, had made a remark that had stuck in Lory's mind. They had said that no one had ever seen Grant Mackinnon lose his temper, that dour he might be, but with an air of total calm about him. She wondered what they would say if they could see him now, his face shadowed in the overhead and dashboard light, the hard planes of his cheeks lending an air of dark strength to already strong features. And the blue eyes were darker, brilliantly dark—frightening. He brought his fist down with a crash on to the dashboard, shaking the vehicle with sudden impact—yet unaware seemingly of any pain from the violence of his action.

And Lory sat very still, feeling as if she had released a tiger from its cage, and with no way of getting it back. Then, with a roar, he started the engine. She pushed her hand on the dashboard, shocked at the sudden movement, as, with a screech of tyres, they rocketed forward. Wide-eyed, thoroughly frightened, she stared at him, at the dark profile as cold as chiselled steel, as he drove down the track. She could see nothing. She didn't know how near they were to the house, and had a nightmare vision of him driving up to it, dragging her into the lounge and denouncing her as a spy in their midst . . .

She saw the gateway as they passed it at a good speed and shouted, above the engine's roar: 'The house—you've passed it——'

'We're not going there!' was the startling answer.

My God! she thought. He's gone mad! Her mouth went dry with fear, but now she was too busy holding on to think of where he might be actually taking her. She tried to think of what there might be in her bag that would serve as a weapon. Keys? Perfume spray? What use would they be against a madman? And then—merciful relief—they were slowing down, climbing, bumping up a steep track. Could she jump out? Her fingers fumbled with the door lock as the thought was translated into the deed, and he heard, and leaned across with his left hand, eyes still ahead to the seemingly impenetrable mist, and pushed her hand away from the lock.

'You'll kill yourself if you try that,' he grated. 'Stay still.'

She froze. And then, quite suddenly, he stopped, and switched off the engine, and a throbbing silence filled the vehicle. 'Now you can get out,' he said.

'But where——' she began.

He didn't answer. Merely leaned over, unclicked the lock and pushed the door open. Then he was out of his own door, slamming it shut, coming round the front—coming for her. Lory looked round desperately. She had no idea where they were, what he was going to do. Could she start the Range-Rover up herself? Could she——

'Right. Get out—please.' The subtle irony, the politeness of that last word, only accentuated the horror of this night-mare situation. Stumbling, knowing it was useless to refuse, Lory, clutching her bag, jumped out, to be steadied by his hand on her arm.

And the swirling mist cleared for an instant—and revealed that they were standing on a cliff top. Rugged rocks marked the edge—and after that a grey blank—with the faint roar of the sea below to tell of the fury that was only a few yards away. Three steps from eternity, she thought, and the newspaper headlines flashed in front of her eyes:

41

'Mystery of Girl's Disappearance from Hebridean Island.'

For a moment, his hand left her arm—and she turned and ran, desperate, fleet of foot—and heard, then felt him behind her, grabbing her again.

'You little fool,' his voice was like steel. 'You could get killed, running off like that——'

'Isn't that better than what you're going to do?' she gasped, terror-stricken, fighting for her life, kicking and struggling.

'Stop it!' his voice was commanding enough to make her pause. 'Why do you think I brought you here? To *murder* you? *Dia!* You're safe enough with me, safer than running away down a rocky mountain. I've come to show you—and tell you things I couldn't tell you down there. Are you going to listen to me—or fight me? The choice is yours, but you'll not win a fight, I promise you that.'

Lory relaxed slightly. His voice was still dark with rage, but her first blind fear had gone. His hands on her arms were holding her, but not with violence.

'I'll—I'll listen,' she said.

'Good. Come back with me.' He turned, and she walked to the top with him again. He put out his arm to restrain her as they reached the edge.

'Here will do.' He sat down on a broad flat rock. 'Sit beside me.' It was not a request, it was an order. And Lory sat down.

Grant Mackinnon turned sideways to face her. 'This is my island,' he said. 'Mine. It's been mine for two years, and I lived here as a child before my parents took me to Canada. I joined the Merchant Navy and travelled the world—until my great-uncle died, and left Creagdubh to me.' He paused. 'I hope you are listening. I don't intend to say this twice.'

'I'm listening.' If he was mad, and that prospect was receding every minute, it was better to humour him.

'Good. I loved this place when I was a lad. I never

wanted to go away, but that was not my choice to make. I love it still, more so perhaps because it belongs to me. I used to come up to this point quite often when I wanted to be alone, and still do. It's not a place for soft people to live on. It's bleak, and the life is hard, and that suits me—and it suits those who live here, or they wouldn't stay either. And no one is going to come here and try and disturb the order of things and tell me what is right or wrong.' His voice, which had been reflective, became harder again. 'And by that I mean you. I don't give a solitary damn for government departments or anything else. *I'm* the laird here, and that's the way it will stay——' There was a pride, almost an arrogance, in his voice. 'If I wish to, I could have you on that plane and off the island tomorrow, make no mistake about that.'

'How could——' she began.

He laughed. 'If I turn you out of Creagdubh House, where would you go? No one else would put you up, I'd see to that.'

Something sparked in Lory. 'That sounds as if you have everyone scared of you! Is that the way you run things?' Once again, she regretted her words instantly. It was something in the quality of the brief silence that followed that made her heart leap in apprehension. She closed her eyes. Why, she thought, don't I keep my big mouth shut?

She heard his deep breath. 'I think,' he said slowly and decisively, each word smooth as stone—and as hard, 'that there is something else you are not telling me. What is it?'

'Nothing.'

'Do you take me for a fool? You have implied that I have the islanders under my thumb. As you haven't yet met any, I would imagine, you must have some reason for that assumption.'

'I'm cold,' she said. 'Can't we go?'

'You're soft, that's why. And I'm not cold. I can sit here all night quite happily, and will do so unless you finish the rest of your story.'

'I have a briefcase with various reports about Creagdubh. One of them was written by the nurse who left here a while ago.'

He had been holding a pebble in his hands, a large one. Lory saw his fingers tighten round it, saw his knuckles whiten, almost as if he were capable of crushing it. 'So that's it,' he said softly. 'I should have known.' It was almost as if he were speaking to himself, and she sensed sudden withdrawal, and she shivered, because there was something very remote about him all of a sudden. Then he stood, and turned towards her, and spoke again.

'We had better be going back now,' he said.

Lory looked up. He was like a stranger again, dark, forbidding. Slowly she stood up too, and followed him away from the jagged edge towards the safety of the vehicle. Questions whirled in her head, but she was too cold to be able to think clearly. Yet she remembered his reaction to her answer, the sudden pressure of his hand on the stone, and she knew that the few simple, seemingly harmless words she had said had sparked off an intense reaction within Grant Mackinnon.

He opened her door and helped her in, slammed it shut and went round to the driver's side. Then he was in again, locking his door, all without speaking. The tension was at snapping point, until Lory could bear it no longer.

'What is it?' she asked.

He looked at her. 'Why—nothing,' he said. 'What should there be?'

'When I told you about—about the nurse, you clammed up.'

'Did I?' He was busy switching on, easing the handbrake off, checking the lights. 'Perhaps I'll tell you when we get back. Just now I have to concentrate on my driving.' And he looked away from her and swung the wheel sharply round. And not another word was said on that journey back to Creagdubh House.

Lory had never imagined how glad she would be to be alone, safely in her warm room, drying the misty drops from her hair with a towel. She sat down on the bed and kicked off her shoes. So much for stupid disguises! She had been here less than six hours and the laird of the island knew exactly who she was, and worse, why she was here. She sighed. She was quite exhausted after the devastating scene on the cliff top—too tired to read any reports. She rubbed her hair vigorously, then shook it free. At least she could be herself now, which was something, although what Edna and Joan would say at breakfast she could not imagine. That was a minor problem. The major one was Grant Mackinnon. He had stopped the Range-Rover at the front entrance, said to her: 'You can get out now, I'm away to park this round the back.' His voice had been quite expressionless, giving nothing away.

'Will—will you tell my friends that I'm safely back? I'm going straight up to my room. I won't have a drink.' She didn't want to tell him she had drunk tea at the Macleods'. She sensed that it might not go down too well with him.

'Aye, if you wish.' And he had leaned over and pushed her door open. 'I'll bring you coffee to your room in a few minutes.'

'Oh no—really——' she was getting out.

'Five minutes.' And before she could reply, he had driven off.

Lory looked at her watch. Nearly fifteen minutes had passed. He had undoubtedly forgotten. She spread the towel neatly over its rail and began to brush her hair—and a knock came at the door. Mouth dry, she called: 'Come in.'

Grant Mackinnon entered and closed the door after him. He carried a cup of steaming coffee, and in the saucer, two biscuits. The room was filled with his presence, and Lory remembered the last time he had been there—when, in a way, it had all started. If she hadn't offered to pay—if she hadn't dropped her glasses—and her bag. If—if ...

'Thank you. Will you put it down on the table, please?'

He did so, then straightened up. 'I have been having a wee chat with Elspeth.' Now how on earth could he make those words sound so menacing?

'Oh! I see.' She looked at him. What next?

'She told me one or two interesting things.' And then Lory remembered her brief conversation with the housekeeper when she had first arrived, and her heart sank.

'She thought it odd at the time that you should compare this island with St. Kilda—but she didn't any more when I told her who you are, and why you're here.'

'But I was only making conversation——' Lory began. It was true, but in the light of what he had just discovered about her, she could hardly expect him to believe it. 'I was merely commenting on the beauty of Creagdubh, and she said how far out it was, and I——' she stopped. What was the use? Everything she said only seemed to make things worse.

'Aye? And you mentioned St. Kilda, did you not? That's a sore point with Elspeth. She had one or two relatives there. So is that what you're planning for us here? To get us all off?'

'Of course not!' But his face was so hard, that she faltered. She put her hand to her forehead, feeling all confused. That was the effect he had on her. 'It's just—I want to see for myself, to talk——'

'You can do that fine well. I'll let you see what life on Creagdubh is like, Miss Stevenson. You're here to work, right? Tell me, do you have fixed hours?' His mouth twisted into a wry smile. 'Are you a nine-to-five person?'

'Of course not! I——' She seemed to be spending all her time saying 'of course not.' 'I work what hours I please——'

'Good. That will suit better. For life on an island of this type is ruled by the weather, and by all sorts of conditions of which you can have no concept. So you will really be able to judge for yourself how things are, will you not? I

46

will see to it myself.'

'But—what exactly do you mean?' she asked, but she already knew, in a kind of growing dismay, mixed with apprehension.

'Can you not guess? I'm here to tell you that I'm going to help you—personally. What better way of seeing life on Creagdubh than with me as your guide?'

'But you have a guest-house to run,' she burst out. 'I can't——'

'You can't accept? Why not? Are you afraid the life will be too tough for you? Aye, well, you have to be fit here. There are no taxis to ferry you around from A to B, only my trusty Range-Rover. Did you know that it's the only motorised vehicle on the island? Better put that in your report. You will be writing reports, won't you? Everyone else walks or rides their bicycles. We have a few here, as a matter of fact, for those who feel energetic enough to pedal their way about. Can you ride a bike, Miss Stevenson?'

'I really don't see——' she began faintly, and his voice went on inexorably:

'Because we can cycle if you prefer it. Or do you not feel it would be dignified enough for one in your exalted position of sociologist?' He made sociologist sound like an obscene word. 'Or aren't you strong enough?'

'I can ride a bike, thank you, and I am quite fit, and I do not get taxis everywhere.' It really was time to assert herself, before this man took over completely. Her hackles rose at the implications of all he said, but if he thought he would frighten her, he had another think coming. He expected her to refuse, to argue, but Lory suddenly thought: Why not? She would see for herself just how things were with or without him. And even with him, she would know things that he might prefer her not to discover. She was adept at sensing atmosphere, of hearing words unspoken, interpreting glances—'And I'm not frightened of work—or of you.' She said the last three words softly, but his mouth quirked.

'Why should you be?'

'Why indeed?' she retorted, cooler now. The worst thing is not knowing what is coming. Well, she knew, at last, and her mind was already busy, planning ahead——

'And for your remark that I have a guest-house to run, that I do, but then I'm one of those fortunate people who need very little sleep. I get up at five or thereabouts in the morning. That is my favourite part of the day—I do not suppose you rise quite so early?' And the dark blue eyes regarded her thoughtfully, intently. He knew what her answer would be, of course.

'Not usually when I'm away from home—but I can do,' she responded sweetly. Anything to wipe away that cynical smirk, that he wasn't quite managing to hide, from his face. 'It's no trouble at all, as a matter of fact.' That was a slight exaggeration, but he had already implied quite enough about her.

'Ah. Good. Would you care to come out with me then in the morning, early?'

She should have known! There was only one answer. 'Why?' she asked. 'What can we possibly see at that time?'

'The island. The bird sanctuary—lots of things. It will clear the way for your real work later, won't it?'

'Er—yes.' How could she get out of this? Short of pretending a broken leg, or pleading insanity, which would be nearer the truth, for only a lunatic would have fallen into so many traps all at once, there was not much Lory could do. 'But what about—er—breakfast?' It was a terribly feeble question, she knew, but it was all she could think of at that moment.

'I'll have a good breakfast ready for you at six. Will that do you?'

'Er—yes.'

'Good. Well, drink your coffee now. I'll say goodnight. Oh—you have an alarm clock?'

'A travelling alarm.'

'Fine. Otherwise I would have given you a call. Goodnight, Miss Stevenson.' And he was gone. Gone, leaving the

48

trace of a smile behind him. Lory flung her hairbrush at the door. It relieved her pent-up frustration somewhat. She looked at her watch. Eleven-twenty. If she was to be up, the sooner she slept, the better. As she prepared for bed, she was already composing in her mind precisely what she was going to say to her father the following day.

The quiet but relentless burr of her small alarm clock roused her from a deep slumber, and she groaned and reached out to switch it off. The entire window appeared to be covered in white paint, and she squinted, and looked again, and saw that it was a thick mist, tendrils of which were teasing themselves into the room even as she looked. Lory sat up, and just for good measure, gave a deep sigh. She would give anything, anything at all for another hour in bed—and then she remembered Grant Mackinnon's face, the lingering smile on his features, and she flung the bed-clothes aside and uttered a few unladylike words.

Fifteen minutes later, at five-thirty precisely, she was dressed in her grey trousers and—after another look at the conditions outside—a warm red polo-necked sweater. She slipped on her flat shoes, picked up her handbag and coat, and opened the door very quietly.

The house slept. Faint snores issued from various rooms and she swallowed her envy of the sound sleepers and crept down the stairs.

She followed her nose to the kitchen. The scent of bacon and eggs is unmistakable, even at so early an hour, and then, reaching a door, the one from which Elspeth must have emerged the previous day, she knocked twice.

'Come away in,' said a deep, unmistakable voice. Taking a deep breath, Lory opened the door.

CHAPTER FOUR

GRANT MACKINNON was standing at a cooker with his back to her. He turned slowly and nodded. 'Good morning. You slept well?'

'Very well, thank you.' Lory would not give him any satisfaction at all, so she straightened her back and smiled brightly. 'I'm sorry I'm a few minutes late. It's very difficult to set those alarms accurately.'

'Is that a fact? I never use one. I tell myself what time I'm going to wake, and it never fails. You should try it some time.' He was busily ladling something that looked like newly mixed cement from a pan into two dishes.

'Well, it would work for you, wouldn't it?' she answered kindly. 'You being so much closer to nature, I mean,' and she put out her tongue at his broad back.

He set one of the plates in front of her. 'Porridge,' he said. 'The bacon and eggs will not be a moment.'

'Oh!' Lory looked down in dismay. 'But I can't eat all this—I mean, the other will be enough——'

'Och no, you need warmth inside you. I insist. Have you not seen the weather? There's a faint ground mist about. It will clear soon, though, I dare say.'

A faint ground mist! Lory looked out of the window and swallowed a retort. Maybe that was all it was to him. He would no doubt call a raging storm a wee drop of rain. She watched in horror as he sprinkled salt liberally on his porridge and passed her the pot. He was watching.

'Thank you.' She did the same, and then added milk from the jug he pushed towards her. Then, well aware that he would be watching her closely even if he didn't appear to

50

be doing so, she began to eat the porridge. Once the initial shock was over—namely, the first mouthful—she began to enjoy it. The milk was as thick as cream, and the salt brought out the full flavour. The only snag was that she was almost too full to move when she had finished. On the other hand, the bacon smelt mouthwateringly delicious ...

Life would never be the same again anyway, not after getting up in the middle of a misty night, so Lory, deciding that nothing much worse could possibly happen now, tucked in to the bacon and eggs. A remark of Edna's came back to her. They always had to diet after a holiday at Creagdubh House. Now she knew why ...

'Good. Toast and marmalade? It will not take a minute.'

'No, thanks.' She waved her hand. 'But you go ahead.'

'Och no, I've had enough. I eat little in the mornings,' he answered, and poured out two cups of strong tea. Lory wondered, fleetingly, what he would consider to be a big meal. He had just polished off, quite effortlessly, a large bowl of porridge, four rashers of bacon, two eggs and three wedges of bread. Perhaps they just grew the men larger in the Hebrides ... Perhaps she was still in bed, and it was all really a dream. But the tea was hot and real enough. And almost strong enough to stand the spoon in.

'Right, we'll away. I think we'll go in the Range-Rover.' He piled the dishes in the sink and took two mackintoshes from the back door. 'This way, Miss Stevenson, if you please.'

She followed him out, and he closed the door firmly behind them and set off across the yard. The whole place had a very eerie look to it, the outbuildings almost completely shrouded by mist, the ground hard as iron beneath her feet, dark moving shadows to each side of them—and silence. Utter silence, save for their footsteps. Grant was dressed in trousers and dark sweater, the trousers tucked into thick wellingtons, and he walked as surefooted as a cat, while Lory followed more slowly, fearful of slipping on the mist-covered ground beneath her.

The Range-Rover stood in a garage which was full of tools and benches and cans of petrol, and he turned round. 'Mind how you go here,' he said. 'Or will I back it out while you wait outside?'

'Yes,' she answered. She was beginning to realize, with a stone-cold certainty, that she was in the wrong job. She should be snugly tucked up in bed now, fast asleep, to wake at eight and catch a nice safe bus to a nice sunny office somewhere ... She sighed. What use were daydreams when this reality was upon her? It only made it worse.

The door slammed, she was in the Range-Rover, and he was turning the huge vehicle round, engine throbbing, lights full on, cutting through the dense greyness for only a few feet before being reflected back. How could he see? He must have eyes like a cat, as well as feet.

'But what can you show me in this?' she said at last, when they were half way down the drive.

'Ach, it will be clear in half an hour—you'll see,' he answered, with the calm certainty of the man who knows exactly what he is about. 'By which time we will be at the birds' nesting place.' And he resumed his concentration on steering a steady course towards the road. Lory sank down further into her seat, thankful for the coat she had brought with her. His motives were as obscure as the ground outside the vehicle. If his intention was simply to let her see how hard and harsh life on Creagdubh could be, he had made an excellent start—but she knew instinctively that there was much more to it than that. But *why*? When he knew what her job was. He should be trying to give her the impression that life on the island was pleasant and well run and that they had no need of sociologists, thank you. Instead of which he seemed, so far, to be going out of his way to make Lory wish she had never come. She drew in her breath sharply. Surely that couldn't be it! And he must have heard it, for he said: 'Is something the matter?'

'No.' She paused. The answer was too abrupt. 'I was just—thinking.'

'Ah. I dare say you have to do a lot of that in your job,' he remarked, and there was nothing in his tone to tell if he spoke sarcastically or not.

'You do in most jobs,' she said. 'Ones that are worth doing, anyway.'

'Aye, that's true enough. And yours would be well worth doing, I dare say, though I wouldn't know a lot about it of course. What exactly is a sociologist?'

'Don't you know?'

'I'd like you to tell me in your own words. There is only so much you can learn from cold print. But you cannot beat the personal angle, can you?' There was no doubt in her mind now. The mockery was oh, so subtle—but it was there all right. Even as she resisted, she felt herself tense up, her heartbeats quicken, because he had a certain effect on her—and seemingly without effort on his part.

'It's the study of people, to put it briefly. People in relation to their environment. Seeing how they live, their reactions to circumstances—everything like that,' she answered. 'But it can't be told in a few words, it's far more subtle than that.'

'I'm sure it is, otherwise you'd have everyone running round telling everyone else what to do, would you not?' he answered. 'And I imagine you'll have done a lot of study-ing?'

'Yes,' she said briefly, and turned away. The skin at the back of her neck tingled, a sure sign of apprehension. She had never met anyone like Grant Mackinnon before. There was hardly any way of fitting him neatly into the pigeon-holes of her mind as she was wont, instinctively, to do with most people she met. And she realized suddenly something she should have known before. All personal dislike apart—and she certainly didn't *like* him—he was an intriguing character. There was firstly this great air of quiet strength about him, and that was not unique, especially in big men—but there was more than that: his manner could be quiet, unassuming, as when he had met the guests from the plane. He could also change swiftly from that to hard implacability—and this was coupled with an intelligence and sensitivity that provided a devastating combination. He was no simple Hebridean, quietly running a guest-house, he was a formidable, powerful opponent. Lory sobered as these thoughts passed through her mind. He was the kind of man who would take on the world if what he was fighting for was right—and he would never admit defeat. It showed; showed in the set of his head, the way he walked and spoke—it showed in his eyes, those eyes that had looked at her the previous night and forced her to tell him who she was. And it showed in his face.

She took a deep breath. Then she would accept the challenge. She would go with him, and let him show her all over the island, and meet the people, and she would not let herself be intimidated by him, because she too was used to getting what she wanted, and somewhere, some time, everyone has to meet their match, and maybe Grant Mackinnon had met his. The fleeting, momentary thought that perhaps it was the other way round, and she had met *hers*, Lory did not even allow to pass through her mind. It was dismissed, to vanish without trace.

Within thirty minutes the mist had disappeared as completely as if it had never been, and Lory was not a bit surprised. They left the Range-Rover parked in a natural lay-by and began to walk up a steep rocky slope. The air was as clear and sharp as a dry wine, and as invigorating. She breathed deeply, preparing herself mentally for any skirmishes that might come, for it was almost as though a running battle were going on. A subtle, polite one, but a battle all the same. Grant walked swiftly, making no concessions to her as a woman, and Lory, determined to begin as she meant to go on, kept up with him. And then they reached the top of the steep slope, and he motioned her to stop, and then pointed.

Sweeping away below them, a sheer black rock face that

ended in jagged rock spears sticking up from the sea, and all down that cliff were thousands of birds, specks of white, nesting in seemingly impossible nooks and crannies, stirring slightly, one or two lifting off and flying away to return moments later so that although most of them appeared asleep, it was as though some guarded their home.

'Speak quietly,' he said, almost in a whisper. 'If we disturb them you'll see a sight you'll not forget.'

'It's fantastic,' Lory admitted. 'I've never seen so many——'

'Ach, this is nothing. These are gulls. I'll take you to see the others in a minute.' He pointed. 'Do you see that island?'

'Yes,' she whispered.

'Do you want to go there now—or later?' He was not asking her if she wanted to go at all, merely when. And how could she admit that in anything other than a boat on a boating lake, she was always seasick?

'Er—I don't know——' she began, playing for time, thinking with faint horror of the huge breakfast she had consumed. 'Later?'

'Och no—we'll away now.' And he looked at her as he said it, as if he had read her mind, and knew of her fear, and was going to take full advantage of it.

'But—what's there?' she asked faintly. Damn the man!

'More birds—different varieties. I go over every so often to make sure everything is in order.' Lory didn't ask what he meant by that, but surely birds didn't need looking after?

'But a boat. Where's the boat?' For a moment the absurd idea that he hadn't got one handy flitted through her mind. Instead he pointed to the right of them.

'This way,' he said cheerfully. 'We'll walk along, away from the gulls, and then it's just a wee scramble down to the shore. We'll maybe catch a couple of fish on the way back—you'd like that? You like fishing?'

It was getting worse by the minute. Without waiting for her answer he was away, striding off through rough heather clumps, over rocks, avoiding the little holes and pits that could snap an ankle with an effortlessness born of long experience. And Lory followed, breathless now, beginning to be irritated—all the more so for having to hide it. Wondering how she could get out of what would undoubtedly be a nightmare trip, beginning to dislike Grant Mackinnon more and more with each stumbling step that passed. But then, when she saw where exactly he expected them to go down, everything else faded into insignificance before the sheer terror of seeing what looked like a vast yawning emptiness before them. He stopped, and looked over, then at Lory.

'Ready?' he said. 'I'll go first and you follow. Then if you stumble, I'll catch you.'

'No,' said Lory.

Grant Mackinnon frowned. 'Och, it's nothing. A bit steep, maybe, but there's a path down. Look.' And he took her arm and drew her towards the stepping off place for eternity.

'No, I'm not going,' she said flatly. 'You go. I'll wait here, or in the Range-Rover until you get back. But I'm not walking off the cliff just like that. Not for you, not for anyone.' And she glared at him, helpless, vulnerable, angry.

His face softened momentarily. He looked, for a few seconds, quite *human*. 'I promise you it's safe,' he said. 'It may not look it, but it's a path—of sorts—and quite dry. See,' and as he spoke he turned, so that he was facing the rigid Lory, crouched down, hands on the edge, and *stepped back*. She had to stop herself from screaming, seeing him in that instant of imagination, vanishing from sight, being hurtled on to the rocks below—but nothing happened. He was there with only his head and shoulders showing, waiting. 'Come on away,' he said. 'Take my hand, turn round— that's it. Nice and easy now.'

Almost as if hypnotized, Lory obeyed, because his words had an intensely soothing quality about them, and while she was to wonder at it later, just then all fear vanished.

56

It was a path—of sorts—as he had said, and once she had actually taken that first fantastic step, it was nothing like as bad as she had feared. Slowly, steadily, he in front, and with his left hand up so that Lory could hold it, he guided her down. There were rocks and huge clumps of prickly heather to grasp, to help her as well, and a steady curving, winding downwards, with only the occasional loose pebble to hurtle away and out, making her tense momentarily. And when they reached the glorious safety of the rocky beach, she dared to look up at their route, and a little shiver of pride ran through her. They'd done it!

He was off again, striding away towards an upturned boat, and Lory, with one final glance at the seemingly sheer cliff, followed. Her right hand still felt the impress of his fingers, and was warm. She shivered again, not from pride or cold, but from something else that she didn't quite understand. How strong he was, how strong his hands—how utterly safe.

'There she is. In you get.' And he picked her up and dumped her in the boat as though she were a sack—a light sack—of potatoes. She sat down abruptly as he pushed the boat out, jumped in, and fitted the oars into the rowlocks. He was facing Creagdubh, Lory was facing the island. The boat was small. It would have held four at a pinch, and it smelt of fish, and creosote, two scents guaranteed not to improve any attempts to stave off seasickness. Lory began to breathe deeply and slowly, counting each breath, concentrating on that, because a friend had assured her once that it was a sure cure for nausea.

'You're looking a mite pale. Does the sea not suit you?' Grant Mackinnon asked, not pausing in his steady rowing, not showing anything on his face, not concern nor mockery, just a quiet blandness that told nothing. But Lory knew. She knew it as surely as if he carried a placard that said the words: 'Tough Luck!' 'You're maybe cold?' he added. 'Put one of the macs around you. That's what they're for—and it will protect your clothes from the spray.'

Silently Lory obeyed. I will not be seasick, she told herself fiercely. I will *not*. He expects me to, and he'd be delighted if I was. He's dragged me out of bed in the middle of the night, dragged me up a cliff, down a cliff, into a grotty little boat that's only fit for a pond, and the sea's bobbing us up and down like two corks, and it's only seven o'clock now, nearly, and he's hoping I'll just give up and go away and leave him and his precious island alone, and I hate him, I absolutely loathe and detest him, and I will not give him the satisfaction of seeing me do just that. He thinks he's in charge of everything, but he's not in charge of me, and he's going to find out and wish he'd never bothered to offer to show me round, because I'm going to enjoy every minute of it even if it kills me! She was not concerned with the sheer illogicality of that last thought, her main concern was of thinking sufficiently positively to sustain her mood of utter determination. And it worked. As they neared the island, she knew she had conquered one thing. She was not going to be sick.

She took a deep breath and smiled at him. 'This is marvellous,' she said. 'Would you like me to take over the rowing?'

He laughed. 'Och no, that's easy. But you'd like to try? You can row back if you like.'

'Fine,' Lory nodded. She had had lots of practice on boating lakes, with various friends or her two nieces, and it would be easy, she knew that. She looked away, leaned over and trailed her hand in the water, which was icy cold. They were nearly there. It wasn't as far as she had thought.

He pulled the boat in as far as possible, and helped Lory out. 'Nice and quiet now,' he said. 'There are thousands of birds all over the place, and there is no sense in disturbing them more than we have to. And besides, some will be hatching out eggs—and they can be pretty fierce if they think you're about to steal their children.'

'But why do they need checking out?' she asked, overcoming her dislike of him sufficiently to ask. He raised one eyebrow as if the question should not have been asked, but answered, mildly enough:

'Why, it's a bird sanctuary. A well-known one, and while I don't claim to be the world's top authority on birds, I can look around and estimate the quantities of birds, of various kinds, the times of the year they arrive—and leave—whether the young ones are doing nicely—all sorts of little things that may not interest a sociologist such as yourself'—here he gave a little bob of the head, almost a bow, and Lory felt her mouth tighten. He didn't exactly tug his forelock, but it was there, the half mocking suggestion of deferring to an expert. He really was impossible! 'And then,' he continued, 'I send off reports to the R.S.P.B. That means,' he added kindly, 'Royal Society for the Protection of Birds.'

'I did know,' she said, managing, with difficulty, not to speak through clenched teeth.

'Ah, you did!' he seemed surprised. 'I'm a member, you see. Well, now that it's all clear, off we go.' They scrambled up a rocky slope, and birds rose in their dozens to circle round them, disturbed, but not unduly so. It was almost, Lory thought, as if they recognized him.

The next hour passed swiftly—and she had to admit that in spite of all her misgivings, she found the trip to the island quite fascinating. During the time, Grant pointed out so many different kinds of birds that her head was spinning. Guillemots—fulmars—gannets—oyster-catchers—eider ducks—fork-tailed petrels. She saw the baby gannets, fluffy white downy creatures, commonly called gugas, perched in their nests on ledges of rock, and Grant explained that they matured slowly and the white down would eventually turn to brown feathers. He spoke with solicitude in his voice, and Lory sensed his genuine concern and involvement with the birds. The ones she found most fascinating were the clumsy puffins with their ungainly walk, their bright coloured, parrot-like beaks, who flapped away at their approach. He pointed to

59

what looked like a rabbit hole in springy turf. 'They build their nests in a kind of long burrow,' he explained, 'but we'll go no nearer. I think we've seen enough for today.'

Lory, bedazzled, agreed. She hadn't wanted to come, but now she knew she would not have missed it for anything.

And then it was time to go. And as they reached the boat, he said:

'You'll be rowing back, then? I'll get out the frame.' He helped her into the boat, pushed it out, and jumped in. From under a tarpaulin he produced a square wooden frame wound round and round with yards of twine, and began to unwind it with care. And Lory saw why. There were several hooks and lines near the end of the twine, and a small lead weight at the very end. He held it poised.

'Away we go, then,' he said. 'I'll tell you when to stop.' Lory began rowing. The only snag was that she had only gone a few yards when she realized that this was nothing like any boating lake she had ever been on. For one thing the water was choppy, and somehow the oars didn't always connect. For another—they didn't really seem to be moving *away* from the island at all. She took a deep breath and began plying the oars with greater vigour.

Some progress was made—at cost to her arm muscles— and Grant Mackinnon sat there with a pleasantly bland expression on his face, and watched her—which didn't make things any easier. It was a great relief when he said: 'Rest your oars. We'll try for a few fish here.' And he dropped the frame into the black depths around them. Within minutes, he was reeling in the line, with not one but three glistening mackerel on, and after that it was simply a question of dropping, hauling in, removing fish, putting the line out again, and repeating the process.

'The sea is rich,' he said, 'and my people are glad of the fish.' The way he said 'my people' was, in a way, quite impressive, and without any trace of arrogance. 'In fact this is one of their main sources of food. But you will see the fishing boats too, when we go to the village. And we share and share alike—that is something that ought to go in your reports. The old do not go without, because they are not able to fend for themselves.' He looked directly at Lory, and the uncompromising deep blue of his eyes was a challenge to her. 'There may be a lesson there for you mainlanders, for do I not read often in the newspapers that old people die alone in their houses and are not found for weeks, or months?'

'I'm afraid it does happen, yes,' agreed Lory. 'But it's because——'

'It is because no one cares. You don't need to tell me,' he said quietly. 'That could not happen here, because everyone is everyone else's neighbour, in the best sense of the word.'

That was something that hadn't been in the nurse's report. Lory tried desperately to recall what had been. The implications were that the laird—Mackinnon—was a tyrant, uncaring of the islanders' welfare, concerned only with his own guest-house, and the running of it. Somewhere, somehow, something did not tie up. And that was why she had to see for herself. And the sooner she re-read that report, the better.

'I'm glad to hear it,' she said. There was nothing else she could say.

He was busy again, and it was as though she were dismissed. Lory was not used to this happening to her. Nobody ever ignored her. But Grant Mackinnon did it quite effortlessly—not rudely, but in quite a decisive way, as if she were so unimportant in his scheme of things that he was able to shut her out of his mind precisely when he chose. She glared at his profile as he leaned over the side, teasing the line up and down slightly, so that the soft feathers in each hook would catch the eye of any passing fish. Totally absorbed in his task, each movement economical, he made a superb picture—that she had to admit in spite of her dislike of him.

'Ach, it's no use,' he said. 'They are gone now.'

'But how did you know where—and when—to stop?'

61

Lory asked, intrigued. 'I mean, you've been pulling them in as fast as you can, and now—nothing.'

He looked at her. 'I just know, that's all,' he answered. 'How does a doctor know where the pain is when you can't say precisely yourself? How does an artist know when he has the exact shade of blue that he needs for the sky?' He shrugged. 'You tell me.' He looked behind him at the glistening pile of corpses—quickly and mercifully despatched by him so that they were not left to gasp for breath—'We have plenty for one day. You may begin the rowing when you are ready.'

Now was the moment to tell him. Now, and not at some point on their return journey when she could no longer carry on. 'I——' she began. 'Er—this rowing is—er—a little bit more difficult than I thought it would be.' There, the confession was out, and although she didn't feel any better for it, at least it was made.

'Is that a fact? Aye, well, it would be, unless you're used to it, and I dare say you'll not have done much of it in London.' Only the ghost of a smile touched his mouth. 'So tell me when you've had enough, and we'll change over. There is no hurry. There never is any haste in the Hebrides, you'll find.' He was busily winding up the twine as he spoke, and did not look at her. Stifling a little sigh, Lory began rowing. There was something else rapidly becoming apparent to her. Blisters! Each pull of the oars was an exquisite torture that rapidly worsened with each stroke. She hadn't realized. It had all looked so simple before—so simple and easy. But that was because he had been rowing. Just as he made scrambling down a cliff face appear like a gentle country stroll. She gritted her teeth and kept going. And going...

'We'll change now. You look tired,' he said in sympathetic tones, just as Lory had reached the point at which she feared she would collapse. 'Stay there. I'll come over.' And he *stood up*. Her eyes widened in horror, visions of them both hurtling into the water flashing before her.

'B—but you——' she began, only then he was sitting beside her.

'Off you go,' he said, and Lory, crouching, clutching both sides of the boat, fell into the other seat. Immediately they seemed to spring forward as if propelled by an engine. The difference between that and her own performance was startling, to say the least. She looked down ruefully at her hands. The palms, just below her fingers, were bright pink and throbbing painfully. She dipped them in the water, and the salt stung them, making her wince.

'Blisters, is it? Ach, had we known, I would have brought gloves,' he said. 'Never mind, they'll soon go.' He wasn't smiling. Not outwardly, that is. But Lory knew. He was enjoying himself hugely. This big powerful man, laird of the island, king of his little community, was fully aware of everything around him, and particularly of her discomfiture. Her inward resolve hardened into steel. This peaceful-looking man was nothing of the kind. He was her enemy. She must not forget that, however he spoke, however helpful he appeared to be. He didn't want her there, and in his own not-too-subtle way, he would probably try and watch her every move. Well, thought Lory, it'll be a battle of wits, as well as a few other kinds of skirmish. And a few blisters aren't going to slow me down.

'But you didn't know I would want to row, did you?' she asked, all sweetness and light. She had a method with men that had come in very useful in the past at ensuring she got her own way. Of course it might not work with *him*. He was an unknown factor in many ways, but a little effort on her part could do no harm. She gave him a warm smile. She could reduce strong men to jelly with that smile—and had done. He returned the smile, affably, and said:

'Er—you'll no' mind me telling you that you have a large black mark on your cheek, will you?'

'Oh!' She fumbled in her bag for the mirror, found it, looked, and swallowed. She remembered brushing her hair from her face just after they had landed on the shore after that seemingly perilous walk down the cliff. 'When did I do that?' she asked, knowing.

'Before we came over the water,' he answered. 'But it's nothing. I only told you now because we're going visiting, and—well——' he shrugged, as if to say he didn't understand the ways of women, and didn't want to.

She rubbed the offending smudge with a handkerchief. 'Thank you,' she said, hating him. All this time, all this *time*, he had been looking at her, and no doubt chuckling to himself—and said nothing. Another little tick went up on Lory's mental black list of his faults. It was quite a long list already. No doubt it would grow with each passing day. The things she was planning to say to her father were becoming clearer every moment. Things like, whose bright idea was it to get me to go to a godforsaken island in the first place? And why didn't you find out that old Mackinnon—dreadful though he might have been—had died and left the place to his even more awful great-nephew, a man who doesn't like strangers—except perhaps as paying guests, and quiet well-behaved ones at that, and who definitely doesn't like sociologists in his little kingdom, even if their motives are the highest? And also . . .

But it was no use. For one thing it would be impossible to speak privately on a telephone that might be eavesdropped upon, for another—and this was the most important thing of all—Lory's father had too great a sense of humour to listen silently to all her grumbles. He would be roaring with laughter before she could get half of it off her mind. She repressed a smile. It would all have to go in a letter. And what a letter it would be! 'Dear Dad, Timetable for first day. Up at five. Climbing and descending cliffs at six . . .'

'We are nearly there now.' Grant's voice broke into Lory's thoughts. 'So brace yourself.' She did so. In some things he knew best. Before he could help her, she had leapt nimbly out of the boat—unfortunately not nimbly enough, for her left foot squelched gently in two inches of cold salty water. Ignoring it—or trying hard to—Lory watched him pull the boat up, ship the oars, lean in and lift out the tarpaulin full of fish and carry it towards her, slung like a black sack over his shoulder.

'I'll away up to the top,' he said, 'with this lot. Then I'll come back for you. Wait here.' Superfluous advice. She had no intention of trying to follow him. She caught her breath as he scrambled up the cliff face, surefooted, swift, no movement wasted. Even one-handed, carrying the fish, he did not hesitate, and the brief thought came to her: he had probably been doing this most of his life. He belonged, much as the birds did; he was a part of the place.

He vanished, then, moments later, was on his way down again. At least, thought Lory, I know why he's not in a kilt today, and she had to repress a grin at the thought. Which meant he must have intended bringing her here. He must have intended it all along. He scrambled down the last few feet and came towards her. 'Okay?'

'Yes. The boat——' she gestured vaguely. 'Is it all right there? I mean, don't you get fierce seas here?'

'Aye, but not in this little bay, not at this time of year. In winter, yes, but then I take the boat into the caves.' It was his turn to point, and Lory followed the direction of his arm along the shore, towards what looked like yet another series of jagged black rocks.

'Caves?' she repeated. 'Where?'

'Can you not see? Come away, I will show you.' He walked away, leaving her to follow. I'm always following him, she thought, only slightly irritated, for curiosity about the caves was overcoming everything else.

And then they arrived, and Lory stopped and drew in her breath sharply, forgetting her wet foot, her blisters, her aching arms—just looking. The jagged blackness was stark and startling; and she was standing looking into the depths from her safe vantage point on the shore, looking inwards to—black emptiness, surrounded by the cruel rocks. There was a frightening, awesome beauty to it all, but strangely, she felt no fear, although caves had made her nervous since childhood, when she had been trapped in one for over an hour with a friend on holiday. Trapped by the sea which had come in too suddenly, leaving them sitting crouched on a rock shelf shouting for help until they thought their lungs would burst.

'Come and have a look inside,' he said, seeing her face.

'No, it's all right—thank you. I can see from here.'

'Ach, but it is better inside. You will see what I mean. Come, there is nothing to fear.' And then he added: 'It is from here that legend says you can see the Moon-dancers.'

The Moon-dancers! She had forgotten all about them. Hardly surprising considering all that had happened since, but immediately fascination caught her, and slowly she followed Grant Mackinnon into that first cave.

CHAPTER FIVE

THE dank air surrounded them as she followed him, and when he stopped, it was so suddenly that she cannoned into him so that he had to turn and catch her. His hard hands were on her arms, not cruel, merely restraining. 'That is it,' he said. 'Be careful. Now—look out to the water. What do you see?'

The sea was framed in the cave mouth, and it looked quite calm and beautiful and in the distance was the island, a dark misty smudge rising out of the water.

'Just the sea,' she answered truthfully.

'Aye, now you do. But it is at night that the things happen—if you believe in these old superstitions, that is.' A delicious trickle of mingled apprehension and mystery ran up Lory's spine. It was the *way* he said it, more than the words themselves.

She whispered, as if fearful of breaking some spell: 'What things happen?'

'Why, the Moon-dancers come. Only in moonlight, only when she is full, and you will see them dancing on the waves, endlessly on and on, seemingly for ever.'

Lory looked, and it seemed to her that she knew what he meant, that in her mind's eye she could visualize the picture. The moon shining down on the water, and flickering on the waves, dancing to some rhythm that no one else could hear, creatures, gauzy, insubstantial creatures, dancing, pirouetting, round and round ...

'What are they supposed to look like?' she said softly—but it was as if she already knew. She had the strangest feeling inside her . . .

'Fairies, kelpies—the little people—nothing human, you understand——'

'No, it wouldn't be. Have you——' she wasn't even bothered that she might be inviting his scorn. 'Have *you* seen them ever?'

'Ach, it's only superstition,' he answered, but what was there in his voice that didn't sound right? 'It's all imagination.'

And Lorry suddenly clutched his arm. '*Have* you?' she repeated, then took her hand away quickly.

He sighed. 'I thought I did—once,' he answered. 'When I was a wee lad. Ach——' she could almost see his careless shrug in the darkness—'it was my imagination, that is all. What else?'

'I don't know. You didn't think so at the time, or you wouldn't have remembered it all these years.'

'Childhood memories last for ever—and are coloured by nostalgia,' he answered. 'Come, you want to go further in? There is supposed to be a way up, through to the cliff top. Can you feel the fresh air?'

There was a slight current, the faintest breath on her cheek, and Lory suddenly shivered. 'No!' she answered, for that was a frightening thought. 'No, I've seen enough, thank you.' She wanted to get out now.

As they made their way to the entrance she remembered something else that the Macleods had told her. What exactly was it? That the seeing of the Moon-dancers—*if* legend were to be believed—heralded good fortune. That was it!

'After you saw—after you *imagined* you saw the Moon-dancers,' she said very casually, 'did anything happen? Anything interesting, I mean?'

They were at the cave mouth now, and Grant stopped and looked hard at Lory as if wondering precisely what she meant. There was a brief silence. Then: 'It was a coincidence,' he said bleakly. 'Come.'

'What was?' she persisted. He began to walk away.

'The day after I *imagined* I saw them, my great-uncle told me he had made me his heir, that Creagdubh would one day be mine,' he said.

He stopped the Range-Rover before they reached the first houses of the village. In strong daylight, the place looked as bleak as the mountains that towered the other side of the dark loch. He leaned over into the back and lifted the fish, now all transferred to a large basket, and got out.

Lory slammed her door to, and walked beside him. 'We'll go and visit old Finlay first,' he said. 'And I'll see what he would like in the fish.'

It was the first house. There was no garden, the cottage straight on to the road—such as that was—and Grant rapped at the door, and then opened it.

A deep voice called: '*Co tha sin?*' and Grant answered: '*Tha mise, Grant.*'

'*Thig a steach.*'

He gestured to Lory. 'He is telling us to go in.'

Lory went into a tiny hallway, with the door open to a room on her right. She blinked, adjusting her eyes to the comparative darkness of the house, then entered the room. An elderly man was sitting by the fire, a huge man, with an old sheepdog asleep at his feet, and he turned his head as Lory and Grant entered, and smiled. And Lory saw that he was blind.

Grant spoke in English. 'I have someone here with me, Finlay,' he said, 'and she has not the Gaelic.'

'Ach, iss that so?' his accent was more pronounced than Grant's, soft and musical. 'You are very welcome anyway.' And he held out his hand, and the dog stirred at his feet, and then went to sleep again.

Lory shook hands. The grip was as firm as a young man's.

'This is Miss Stevenson, Finlay,' Grant said. 'She is here from England to see how we are all going on on Creagdubh.

69

Now will I leave her with you while I go and attend to my business in the village?'

'Aye, of course you will. Away you go, then.'

'I'll leave some fish in your kitchen. I'll do them when I get back.'

'Good. Good. I was just now saying to Anna that it would be nice to have a piece of fish for our tea.' The dog wagged her tail at hearing her name, looked at Lory, clearly decided she was a friend, and closed her eyes again. Grant went into the kitchen with the basket, and came out a few moments later. He looked at Lory, nodded, and left.

'Sit you down, Miss Stevenson,' the old man said, 'Pull up a chair near the fire, and in a minute I will make for you a cup of tea.'

'Thank you, but shall I make it?' she enquired gently.

'Ach no, I am used to it. I manage very well. So you are here to see how we are all going on? That is very nice of you indeed.' And he nodded, the sightless eyes closed, his gnarled hand stroking the dog as he leaned forward to it. He had a strong face, full of character, a large beaky nose, a mane of white hair. It was, Lory decided, the face of a man you could trust. So what was she doing here under false pretences? Grant had merely said that she was here from England to see 'how we are all going on on Creagdubh'. A statement which the old man had accepted without comment. And yet the blind can sometimes see more clearly than those with sight. What was he thinking, this old man, as he sat by his fire stroking his dog?

'I am a sociologist,' Lory said. 'I'm staying at Creagdubh House for a week or so, and I want to go round the island and talk to everyone and see how they manage——'

'Manage?' Finlay interrupted. 'I am not so sure that I understand what you mean, Miss Stevenson.' He was frowning. 'We manage very well here. Did someone think that we did not?'

Her heart sank. Things had taken a sudden, unexpected turn. And she seemed to remember a certain expression on

70

Grant's face just before he had left. It hadn't been her imagination. He had brought her here first for a reason. And where would he be now? Talking to other islanders, putting ideas in their heads? A little tingle ran up her spine. If that was the way he wanted to do it, all right, she didn't have much choice. He knew everyone and she didn't. She would just have to play it by ear.

'Oh no,' she answered. 'But it's just that small communities like this one are interesting to those on the mainland. Life is so different, isn't it? I mean, you don't have transport, or buses——' she faltered, the absurd image of a London double-decker bus being driven down the narrow track coming irresistibly into her mind—'and,' she managed to collect her wits again, 'there aren't any shops, are there?'

'Shops? What would we be wanting with shops? We have the post office!' He said it proudly, as if that explained everything.

'The post office,' she repeated faintly, remembering the tiny cottage with the words above a very small window.

'Aye. We can get all we need there. And the boat comes every week—that is if the weather's not too severe—and there is the plane too.' He nodded. 'Aye, well, we'll have a cup of tea and then talk. I like a cup of tea in the morning, and I dare say Grant will be gone a while.' He stood, using his left hand on the mantelpiece to steady him. The dog, Anna, clearly well used to her master, moved away as swiftly as she was able and curled up under a wooden settle by the window.

'Are you sure I can't help?' asked Lory.

'No, lassie. It's kind of you to offer, but I manage very well, as you will see.' He went out to the small kitchen, and Lory heard the clatter of a kettle against a tap, the plop and hiss of gas, and then a cupboard opening. She looked around the room, furnished very sparsely—clearly for practical reasons, for it was not large. A row of well-cared-for plants were lined up in pots on the window-ledge, beneath it on a low table was a modern transistor radio looking strangely out of place in the otherwise old-fashioned room. There was the very old wooden settle underneath which the dog lay, her own and Finlay's chairs, and a sideboard on which stood a pile of books. Books! She stood up, consumed with curiosity, and went over to them.

'May I look at your books?' she called.

'Aye. Maybe you'll wonder what a blind man is doing with reading matter? Grant brings them for me, and one of my neighbours reads to me in the evenings.'

So they were Grant's. Lory picked up the top two, interested to see what Grant would lend this old man. One was a James Bond thriller, the other a book of poems by Rossetti. Intrigued by this contrast, Lory looked over the rest, to see a mixture of the new and the old, spy stories, science fiction alongside Conan Doyle.

The voice floated in from the kitchen, followed by the man, as Finlay returned with two beakers. 'Ach, I can see you are surprised. Did you think an old man would only read old books?'

He could 'see' she was surprised—but Lory was ceasing to be astonished herself at anything to do with this dignified islander. 'No,' she answered, 'but I like books so much myself that I always find other people's very interesting, and to see a James Bond next to a book of poems—well, it was quite a contrast.'

Finlay laughed, put the two beakers on the mantelpiece, and sat heavily down in his chair, where Anna immediately joined him, slinking across and curling up at his feet. 'Aye, that it is, but he knows what I like, does young Mackinnon.' His sightless eyes seemed to look through and beyond her. 'Now what is it that we were talking about? Don't forget your tea, Miss Stevenson.'

'Would you call me Lory?' she asked.

'If you like. Lory, that is a nice name. And so you're a sociologist, are you? That means you're interested in human behaviour. Tell me, don't you sometimes feel as

72

though you're going round a zoo—a human zoo—looking at the inmates? That is how it strikes me a sociologist would behave.'

Lory swallowed. She was beginning to realize why Grant Mackinnon had brought her here first. She was talking to someone of powerful intellect, a deceptively quiet man who seemed to have the habit of stripping words to see what lay behind them. That certain expression on Grant's face became even clearer. 'It's not like that really,' she said gently, and picked up her hot beaker. 'I mean, I don't regard myself as someone going round a zoo——' she faltered. He had conjured up an irresistible picture—'but I am interested in people, naturally—it wouldn't do not to be in my work, would it?'

'And our little island interests you, then, does it? So what do you think of our laird?'

'Mr. Mackinnon?' How did she answer *that*? 'He seems very—er—helpful.'

'Ach, is that all you can say? I sensed that all was not well with you when you came in. Was I mistaken?'

She wanted to say—no, you weren't—but something stopped her. She had to be very careful. 'I don't think he likes sociologists,' she said, truthfully.

'Is that a fact? He's a man of very strong opinions, is Grant Mackinnon. And yet he lets you stay at his house, though.'

'He didn't know I was a sociologist when I went there,' said Lory, and was startled when the old man burst into hearty laughter.

'Oh, forgive me,' he said, when he could speak. 'But I can see it all now.' He wiped his eyes on a handkerchief, reached for his beaker and took a deep swallow. 'Ach, that's better. Is the tea to your liking, Lory? Or would you need some more sugar?'

'It's fine, thank you.' She wished that she didn't feel out of her depth, a disconcerting sensation. There was worse to come.

'Are you pretty?' asked Finlay suddenly. 'I know you're young, but are you as beautiful as your voice?'

'I don't——' Lory began. How did you answer a question like that?

'Come here, child, let me see for myself.' Curious, Lory went nearer to him and crouched down at his command. The gnarled old fingers sped gently over her face, like a sculptor seeing his handiwork through touch.

'Ah yes,' the old man let out a sigh. 'You have good features, you have youth and beauty on your side. But Grant is like his great-uncle in that respect. He does not like women.'

Lory slid back into her seat. Nothing that Finlay said should come as a surprise, she knew. But even so, his words had the ability to shock.

'Why?' she asked.

'Why?' the old man shrugged. 'I do not know. How does anyone know what makes a man as he is? You will have a struggle on your hands with him, that's all I can tell you. He brought you to me for a reason, and I think I know what that reason is.'

'I wish I did,' said Lory, now thoroughly confused.

'Then I'll tell you. We are simple folk here—simple islanders—and we don't like strangers coming to tell us what to do——' he held up his hand at Lory's indrawn breath—'No, wait, I know what you are thinking, I can read your mind as surely as you can read a book—you are thinking that you are not really here to tell us what to do, you are here to look around, talk to us, that is all. That is how you see it, and I am sure you are a sincere woman, for I can feel the vibrations, and they are right.' He paused, but this time Lory could not have interrupted for the world. Strange fascination held her transfixed, as his steady words poured out. 'But things have a habit of changing subtly, and you will no doubt write what you have to write, and people will read it, and sometimes, when things get down on paper, they seem different. And we do not want any change

74

here, we are happy as we are. Does that seem strange to you?'

'I don't know,' Lory answered. There was no sense in pretending anything with this man. 'I've only been here a day—less than a day really, and already I can feel the change in *me*—but I don't know what it is.'

He gave a short laugh, his cheeks creasing, his hand slapping his knee. 'Ach, you will change even more before you are through, you'll see. You will find that——'

And then he stopped, because the outer door opened, and Grant Mackinnon came in, and instantly the atmosphere altered. Lory desperately wanted the old man to finish the sentence, for she sensed he had been about to say something very significant, but she knew now that he would not.

'Well,' said Grant, looking from Lory to Finlay and back again, 'I see you're enjoying a nice chat.' And there was no irony in his voice. Nothing—save that cynical half smile on his face that might or might not have been Lory's imagination.

'Och yes,' said Finlay. 'Come away and sit down. There is tea in the pot.'

'I've just now had one at the Kilmores',' answered Grant. 'Thank you all the same. I'll be taking Miss Stevenson there next, but first I'll do your fish. Come into the kitchen, Miss Stevenson, and I'll show you how to fillet a mackerel. You'll maybe find it interesting.'

'Och, why so formal?' asked Finlay. 'Miss Stevenson indeed! When she is a guest in your house too.'

Grant looked directly at Lory, who said, confused: 'Please call me Lory.'

'You're very kind—Lory. I would not have done so otherwise, of course. I hope you'll call me by my name.' And he stopped, and waited, and he wasn't laughing, not quite.

She swallowed. 'Yes, of course.'

He went into the kitchen, and Lory followed. 'There now,' said Grant. 'I take this knife, so——' and he picked

up a wickedly sharp kitchen knife, 'and I do this—so——'
and he deftly slit the fish down the centre and Lory
watched, fascinated, despite herself, at the speed and skill
of it all, at the way the neat fillets of fish were deposited on
a plate, and the bones—all the bones—were wrapped into
newspaper.

'That's it,' said Grant, rinsing his hands. 'You want a go
next time?'

'I don't think I——' Lory began.

'Och, you never know till you try. Children learn this job
here as soon as they can be trusted with a knife. We don't
have our fish pre-packed and frozen and neatly filleted for
us, remember, we have to do it ourselves. So you might as
well learn for yourself, and then when you write about it,
you'll know exactly what you're writing about, won't you?'
And he picked up the newspaper bundle and strode into the
living room, leaving Lory, as usual, to follow him.

'That's it now, Finlay,' said Grant. 'The fish is on your
sink. Enough for two meals, I'd say. Is there anything you
need before we go?'

'No, I'm fine. Just fine. Thank you for the fish. I'll see
you again soon, will I?'

'You will. Goodbye now, Finlay.'

'Goodbye, Grant—goodbye, Lory. Thank you for
coming.'

He shut the door quietly after them, and as they went
into the narrow street, Grant said: 'Away to the Kilmores'
now. Got your notebook?'

She was startled at the question. Had he seen? Did he
imagine her scribbling frantically at Finlay's? She hadn't,
of course. It would have seemed rude. Yet she longed to
make notes. 'Yes, I have,' she answered. 'But I don't——'

'You'll need it where we're going,' he cut in. 'Because
you'll see too much to remember.' It was a cryptic remark
to say the least, but more annoying was something else.

'Do you always interrupt people?' Lory asked sharply.
'You rarely let me finish a sentence, you know.'

'Is that a fact?' He turned his dark amused gaze on her as they walked along past the cottages—curtains twitched at some as they passed—and began to climb a hill, away from the loch. 'Then maybe you should speak a little quicker.'

'You're the one who's always saying there's no hurry,' she pointed out, reasonably enough, and was annoyed when he began to laugh.

'So I did,' he agreed. 'So I did. You'll have to forgive me, then—Lory—won't you?'

She didn't like the way he said Lory, but there wasn't much she could do about it. She sighed, concentrating on treading safely up the rough pitted track. She looked behind her once, and was surprised to see how high they'd come. Ahead of them, at the top of the hill, was a large sprawling house, and at the side a long line of washing blowing in the breeze. Several sheep followed their progress with mild interest, and, as they neared the house, Lory saw several hens pecking and scratching at the stony ground. And then, as she looked towards the door, it opened, and out poured what seemed like dozens of children. For a moment she wondered, confusedly, if this was the schoolhouse and her sense of direction had gone astray, and then she realized two things in quick succession. One, it was Saturday, and two, what had seemed like lots of children was in fact six. They came towards her and Grant in a mad rush helter-skelter, scrambling down, scattering squawking hens, shouting merrily. Grant stopped and scooped up the nearest two in his arms as they reached him. Two girls of about seven and, Lory realized, identical twins.

'All right,' he said, laughing. 'Don't frighten Miss Stevenson now. She is not used to such noise.' Six pairs of eyes were immediately turned on her, six tousled dark heads became still, and she was able to take stock. A boy of about two, the last to arrive, stood looking solemnly at her with thumb in mouth, then another boy about five, a girl

77

the same age—surely not more twins? They were very much alike, and of a size, and another boy, bigger and stronger looking, probably eight or nine.

Grant rattled off names, nodded, because of his full arms—'Donald, Callum, Mairi, Iain, Jeannie—and Morag.'

'Hello there, come away in.' A woman was standing in the doorway watching them, a woman possibly in her early thirties, with dark hair the same as her children's, wearing a shapeless blue smock that didn't hide the bulge. She smiled as the little crowd neared her, and said to Lory: 'I tried to keep them quiet, but they were so excited to see this visitor that Grant was bringing.' Then she held out her hand. 'I'm Jean Kilmore. Please come in.'

'Thank you.' Lory shook hands with the woman, liking her instantly. Inside was chaos, nappies piled up in the corner, toys and teddies scattered over the thinly carpeted floor, a smell of burning milk coming from the kitchen, and yet, over all, an atmosphere of warmth and welcome.

Grant deposited the twins on the floor, and their mother said: 'Get your coats on and go outside and play for a wee while.' She looked at Lory. 'Please sit down, I'll put the kettle on. It's so nice to have another woman to talk to.'

Grant was watching her again. Lory sensed it even when she wasn't looking directly at him. Then he spoke. 'I'll away back to the house, Jean. It's all right for Miss Stevenson to stay a while, is it? She'll not be in your way?'

He speaks as if I'm a piece of furniture, thought Lory.

'Och no, that's fine. Off you go, then. My regards to Elspeth—and tell her thank you.'

'Aye, I will. I'll see you later, Lory.' And with that, he was gone. She heard him talking to the children outside, and then their voices faded away.

'He's very kind,' said Jean Kilmore. 'Elspeth is always sending things for the wee ones. This morning he brought some blankets and sheets—the way mine get through them you'd think they were paper.'

'How many children have you?' asked Lory gently. 'Six?'

'Yes, and another on the way.' She patted her stomach. 'But I wouldn't be without them, any of them. I know what some think in the village, but it's only because they're old. They've forgotten what it's like being children. My husband is away now with the boat. He'll be back tonight, I hope.' She sighed. 'And you are here to see what we are about, are you not?'

'Is that what Grant said?' Lory asked.

'Aye. Well, it's a hard life, right enough, but I'd not change it. Not me.'

She went to the kettle, which had started to rattle up and down on the coals, and poured boiling water into a teapot. 'That will be ready in a minute.' She sat down again. 'And you're from London? What is it like there? I have never been. Is it as busy as they say?'

And Lory found herself telling the other woman about her life in London, and answering questions about her work, and they drank their tea and ate home-made oatcakes with butter and jam—and the time sped by like magic so that it was quite a shock to hear Grant's voice at the door, and then to see him enter the room. And then Lory realized with dismay that she knew no more about Creagdubh than she had before.

'Och, it was lovely talking to you,' said Jean Kilmore. 'I have so enjoyed it. Please come again.'

'Yes, of course,' said Lory, smiling, hiding her dismay. She was getting nowhere, nowhere at all.

The children accompanied them down the track for a way, then said their farewells, and Grant said to Lory: 'Well now, you're seeing island life, and what do you think of it so far?'

'Interesting,' answered Lory with firmness. He was not going to get the better of her. 'But I can't really say I've found out a lot.'

'Is that a fact? Aye well, you will do soon. This is your

first day, remember. You can never do much on the first day. There is settling in to be done—and things like that. You will soon find your feet and remember all the questions you want to ask my people.' There it was again. 'My people,' said in such simple tones that it had the power to impress.

'Where are we going now?' she asked, biting back the instinctive answer that had come to her—that she had indeed been extremely active since very early morning—because such answers might well tempt him to test her stamina still further, and she was trying hard to hide any traces of tiredness. Her foot had dried, thank goodness. The blisters throbbed on her palms, and her shoulder muscles ached. But she wouldn't tell *him* that.

'Och, we'll away back to the big house and I'll give you a wee lesson in filleting fish'—so he hadn't forgotten!—'then lunch.'

Food! She was starving. She swallowed hard. 'Oh, good.' But there was another question that had to be asked. 'And then what happens?'

Grant seemed to hesitate, then looked at her speculatively. She wondered for a moment if she had another smudge on her face, but Jean would have told her, surely? 'What is it?' she asked, when she could bear the suspense no longer.

'Well——' it was a slow, long-drawn-out 'well,' 'I'm in the middle of doing some work at a wee house at the other side of the island, and the people are a bit strange—they're not so keen on "foreigners," as they call everyone who doesn't actually live here——' Lory's ears pricked up. He didn't *want* her to go! Which was odd, considering his apparent desire to let her see and meet everyone. Yet this could be the type of encounter she needed.

'I'll be very quiet,' she said calmly, mentally crossing her fingers.

'You will? Hmm, I could pretend you were helping me, of course. They'd accept that. They'd not question me having an assistant——'

'Then I'll help you! Er—what are you actually doing?'

'Just some minor repairs. It won't be too hard for you?' The concern in his voice didn't ring true, but Lory ignored it. She was extremely capable at many tasks, believing herself better able to do household repairs than most men.

'I doubt it,' she answered crisply as they reached the parked Range-Rover. A good lunch, followed by a good wash, would freshen her up immeasurably. Grant Mackinnon might be a formidable opponent, but she was gaining confidence with each hour that passed. It was something to do with the positive thinking she practised, she assured herself. Even that half glimpsed smile of his as he strode away to his door didn't shake that feeling. Not until much later. And then it was too late.

CHAPTER SIX

THE wee house, as Grant had called it, nestled snugly in a hollow with the hills behind it, and the sea in front of it. As they left the Range-Rover and began to scramble down the rocky ground, Lory considered the wonderful view briefly, and then concentrated on keeping her footing. Here she would find out what it was all about, she felt sure. The very fact that he hadn't really wanted her to come was sufficiently interesting to arouse her curiosity, and although she had assured him that she would be very quiet, she had no intention of standing silently around. Her powers of observation were very keen. She wondered what manner of people these were who so resented 'foreigners.' And why.

'Nearly there,' his voice floated back encouragingly. He was ahead of her—as always—not looking back to see if she could manage, but that no longer bothered Lory. She was getting quite used to it. The track—such as it was—petered out, and they had to jump several feet, and here at last he did turn and offer her his hand to assist her. They were on level ground now, and she looked along towards the house and shivered slightly. Everything was grey—the stones, the roof, even the window frames. How bleak and desolate it seemed! Not even the smoke blowing merrily from the chimney could take away that first sombre impression. And what could Grant be doing here? Painting the inside grey as well, perhaps? He looked at her, as if reading her thoughts.

'They won't bite,' he remarked pleasantly. 'Don't look so scared.'

'I wasn't!' she retorted, and then saw that he was laughing at her, and closed her mouth. She would not start any arguments with him. She would *not*.

He had brought some fish, wrapped in newspaper, and Lory remembered her brief lesson in the kitchen before lunch, watched not only by Grant, but by Elspeth—a fact which had caused her to grit her teeth and try, really try, to get everything correct. For of one thing she was quite sure, Elspeth did not approve of her, not one little bit, and she felt as if she had to show the housekeeper just how efficient she could be, although she wasn't sure why. Grant had nodded with mild approval at her first solo attempt to gut a mackerel. 'Aye, not bad,' he had said. 'I dare say you'll improve with practice,' and then he had taken the knife from her and done the remaining fish, as if to show her just how simple it was for an expert like him.

She looked at him now as he knocked on the door—not grey but black—and she thought: You're an arrogant devil when you want to be. And her skin tingled at the sight of him as he stood there, head slightly cocked as if listening for footsteps. All male, big, strong, self-sufficient—and so sure of himself that he did not care one jot for her opinions on his island. That was the almost frightening thing. It was as if he knew he was right, and that was all there was to it. And she had dared to strike him. Seeing him now, she was amazed at her own temerity. He looked powerful enough to fell an ox, if he chose—and *she* had hit him!

She almost jumped when the door opened a crack, so engrossed had she been in her thoughts, and a voice said softly:

'Och, it's himself.' The crack widened, the door was opened fully, and Grant said:

'Aye, it is. I have come to finish the jobs, Mrs. Campbell. May we come in?'

The woman was a pale shadow, clutching at the door as if it would support her. Her eyes caught Lory's, and she looked quickly away and back at Grant.

'Miss Stevenson has come to help me,' he said, and Lory

noticed for the first time how gentle his voice was, not at all as when he spoke to her.

'Aye, come in now.' But she wouldn't meet Lory's eyes. Inside Lory looked discreetly around her, and was astonished at the contrast with the house's exterior. A peat fire glowed silver and red in the high black polished grate, and everywhere was colour, from the rich dark woods of the sideboard and table to the brightly embroidered cushions on the cottage suite. The floor was of red-painted stone, and a handmade rug of gold and brown lay in front of the fire, giving emphasis to that black grate.

And then Lory looked at Mrs. Campbell, and smiled at her. It was almost a physical shock to see how thin she was, thin and frail, with wispy grey hair framing a pale worried face. She wore a shapeless black dress covered by a brown pinafore, and on her feet were heavy black shoes, old and cracked, but highly polished. She gave a quick brief smile in return, then looked away anxiously towards a door. 'I'll away and tell John,' she said. 'Please sit down.'

'Och, I'll start work if that's all right with you,' said Grant cheerfully. 'And Miss Stevenson will help me. She has come to visit Creagdubh for a wee while. You'll no mind me bringing her?'

'Why—no, of course not. Er—excuse me——' and she was gone, melting away like a shadow, out of the room. Lory was disturbed. No wonder Grant had not wanted her to come. She ached to tell this pale grey creature not to be frightened of her, but of course she couldn't. She wondered what Mr. Campbell would be like. A big brute of a man who kept his wife in that nervous state? It seemed highly likely . . .

'Right, Lory, this way.' She followed him through into the kitchen, and out of the back door. Everywhere was clean and polished—and quite colourful, a surprising contrast to not only the exterior, but the woman of the house herself.

Outside at the back, Grant pointed to a ladder propped against the wall. 'I'm finishing off the roof,' he told Lory, and she saw a pile of slates neatly stacked on the rough stony ground. 'But I don't expect you to climb the ladder, don't worry. You'll maybe be good enough to pass me slates as I need them?'

'Yes, of course.' She wrenched her mind back from puzzling over the Campbells, and to the task in hand.

'You look—disturbed,' he said softly.

'Yes,' she said, and no more.

'Aye, well, I'll tell you afterwards. Not now.' And with that he steadied the ladder and began to climb. He had not far to go. Although the cottage had two storeys, the ground at the back was higher than in front, so that he was within reaching distance even when at the roof level.

The next hour or so was busily occupied in passing up slates, one at a time, and an arm-aching task—added to her already protesting muscles—it was. But Lory, determined not to let him know, kept a brightly alert smile on her face, while inwardly cursing. She knew now what that smile of his had meant! And she had fallen very nicely into a little trap.

The wind had risen, and whistled round them as they worked, and she thought that she had never been so uncomfortable in her life, and longed to sit down with a cup of tea. What wouldn't she give for a lovely hot cup . . .

'I have the kettle on just now, Grant. Will you have a wee *strupach*?' The little voice floated from the back door as if in answer to her prayer, and Grant shouted down:

'Thank you, Mrs. Campbell, that would be nice. I'm nearly finished now.'

The sounds of hammering ceased, and the ladder wobbled as he came down. He looked at Lory. 'Okay?' he said.

'Fine,' she agreed, wondering if her smile looked as gritty as it felt.

'Good. You're a very efficient assistant—you know,' he added thoughtfully, as he reached her, and stood looking down at her from his superior height, 'you didn't come to Creagdubh to work, did you? Not this sort of work anyway,' and he jerked his head in the direction of the roof. 'But you see, you did want to find out how we lived here, and—well,' a shy smile that didn't deceive her for one instant, 'there is only one way to really find that out, and that's to be here—with me—isn't it?'

There were things she could have said—several things—but Lory, with a considerable effort of will, restrained herself. For in one way he was right, and it was the way that mattered. She would never have come here to the Campbells' without him—she would not even have known of their existence. There could be more places too, and only by seeing all she could would she be able to build up a picture of Creagdubh in its entirety. 'You're quite right,' she agreed sweetly. 'And please don't worry about making me *work*,' she emphasised the last word deliberately, 'it all goes down to experience—and that, in a way, is what my job is all about. And it's interesting to see what kind of life *you*, as the laird, have.' And she turned away, and walked towards the back door. *That* might give him something to think about.

Mr. Campbell had appeared, and seemed to be busy hammering nails into a wooden frame when they went in. He looked up, and then nodded.

'This is Lory Stevenson, Mr. Campbell,' said Grant, and the man held out a hand to her and said in a slow, gentle voice:

'I am pleased to meet you, Miss Stevenson.' He was like his voice, a gentle-looking, apparently slow-moving man, and she took to him instinctively. Now why had Grant said they didn't like foreigners? The only thing they seemed to suffer from was shyness, and that was no fault. Mrs. Campbell could be heard clattering in the kitchen, and then she appeared with a loaded tray with tea, and a plateful of mouthwatering-looking scones, and any need for polite small talk was lost in the ceremony of handing round tea and plates. Lory sensed the desperate shyness that filled them both, and longed to help them. And then she saw something that she should have noticed when she had first entered, but for some reason had not. A piano stood in the corner of the room, an old one, with candelabra attached, as lovingly polished as the rest of the furniture, and Lory, looking at it, said: 'Oh, you have a piano. How lovely! Do you play, Mrs. Campbell?' It was a casual question, made more to fill an imminent gap in the conversation than anything else, but it was to have far-reaching consequences. In a way, it was to help affect the whole of Lory's life.

Mrs. Campbell's face changed. She almost brightened, and Lory marvelled at the difference in the woman. 'Yes, I play,' she said, 'and my husband plays the violin. Are you interested in music, Miss Stevenson?'

'I had lessons when I was younger, but I'm sadly out of practice now,' admitted Lory. 'But it's like riding a bike, I suppose. Once you've learned, you never really forget. May I look at it?'

'Of course.' The woman followed her to the piano and opened the lid. The keys were almost yellow with age, and Lory's fingers itched to touch them.

'Would you like to try it?' Mrs. Campbell said, as if sensing this.

'If I may—but I'm not very good.' The piano stool was produced as if by magic from underneath. Lory, scarcely aware of Grant's presence—he was keeping very quiet—sat down and ran her fingers gently over the keys, and then, hesitantly at first, but gaining confidence with each moment that passed, she played one of her favourite pieces, a Chopin waltz. The tone was superb, and when she had finished she turned to her hostess and said: 'It's absolutely beautiful, and the pitch is perfect.'

'Aye, my mother left it to us,' Mr. Campbell said, coming over to where his wife and Lory were. 'And Finlay taught me how to tune it a good few years ago—you'll not have met him, I don't suppose?'

'She has,' said Grant. 'This morning just. What is it he plays now, John?'

'Ach the pipes, of course—and the fiddle too, like myself.'

'Aye, that's it,' Grant said thoughtfully. 'But I dare say he's a bit out of practice now. There's no' many play in the village any more.'

In a way Lory sensed she was out of things, but she was content to listen, and to look at the beautiful instrument before her. She had started something—she was not sure what—and instinct told her that there was a reason for Grant's intervention—and she was beginning to sense what it was.

'Aye, well, that's the way of it,' John Campbell said. 'There is the radio now, and people do not have to make their entertainment any more—they have it made for them.' And then there was a pause, and in that pause Lory, some sixth sense forcing her, said:

'Will you play something, Mrs. Campbell?'

For a moment she wondered if she had done wrong, and then Grant, quite quietly, and very gently, for him, said: 'Aye, Mrs. Campbell, will you?'

And Lory looked up, and caught an anguished expression on the woman's face, and caught her breath. 'Oh, please,' she said, 'not if you don't want to.'

Mrs. Campbell smiled. 'It's all right,' she said. 'Of course I will.' And she sat down in the seat Lory had vacated. Lory picked up her tea and her scone and very quietly sat down in her chair.

What followed was not mere music. It was sheer magic; it was poetry. The tune, a simple one, that Lory didn't recognize, was straightforward enough, but the woman put her heart into it, and Lory sat unmoving, her tea growing cold. Once she glanced at Grant, and caught something on his face as he looked across at Mr. Campbell, and again it was as if she were not really part of the scene, but a spectator. Yet she was not uncomfortable. Without knowing why, she had done something important, and she intended to find out exactly what it was from Grant, afterwards.

The tune was over, the sounds died away, lingering on the air for several seconds before vanishing, and Mrs. Campbell got up from the piano and left the room. Immediately her husband, after a brief glance at Grant, followed.

'What is it?' Lory whispered, and Grant turned to her.

'Nothing,' he answered, his voice equally low. 'I'll tell you later.'

'But she was crying,' whispered Lory, disturbed.

'I know. But it's all right.' Then, in a louder voice, he called: 'We'll away and finish the roof.' He stood up, putting his cup and saucer on the mantelpiece.

He led the way through the kitchen and out of the back door, and motioned Lory away from the house. When they were sufficiently far to be entirely out of earshot of anybody within, he turned to her.

'You want to know what you have done?'

'Yes, of course. I thought—it all seemed so right, somehow, and then——' she shrugged, anxiety colouring her voice. For the moment they were no longer enemies. Grant's veiled hostility seemed to have disappeared, yet she waited for his scorn, not trusting to her instinct any longer, feeling thoroughly confused.

'Yes, it was. You have—innocently, and without knowing exactly what you were doing—broken a barrier. You have done Mrs. Campbell good.'

'But I—she was upset——' Lory began.

'Yes. Now I'll tell you why. It's all right, they cannot hear us, and even if Mrs. Campbell looked out of a window, I am just showing you the view from here,' and he pointed towards the sea, as if telling her of it. 'Twenty-five years ago their only son, a boy of ten, died, and Mrs. Campbell, who was lively, beautiful and young, changed into that grey ghost of a woman you saw just now. There was nothing anyone could do to help, John least of all, and he is the kindest and most understanding man in the world. She just shut herself away here, and would not see anyone—anyone at all. She never goes to the village, she never leaves the house. She sits and embroiders and sews and polishes the furniture all day and every day.'

Lory shook her head. 'Oh no,' she said, 'oh no.'

'Oh yes, it's true. I am the only outside person she has spoken to for a quarter of a century, and only because I am the laird, and because her son was a school friend of mine. I come here every week, for one reason or another, and I do little jobs for them that sometimes don't need doing at all, and sometimes I will stay for an hour or two while John goes to the village for their supplies, for he does not like leaving her alone.

'Apart from her sewing, the only thing she lives for is music. That has possibly kept her sane, although I wouldn't know, I am not a psychiatrist.' He paused, and looked at Lory. 'And if I had told you what to say, you could not have done better than you did. I really did not want to bring you—except to see you working—and then I thought, why not? It can do no harm, and it might do good—and I think you have done more good than you know. Will you come again with me?'

'Yes.' She did not hesitate in her answer.

'Good. Come, I'll finish the roof.'

There was nothing for Lory to do except wait at the foot of the ladder, and she had time to think. It was almost as if a truce existed between her and Grant, and she was surprised to know how pleasant a feeling it was. She wondered how long it would last. She was soon to find out.

It was later that evening, in her room, that the idea came to her. Sitting by the table at her window after dinner, Lory cupped her chin in her hand and thought over the events of the day before putting them down on paper.

So much had happened, and she was exhausted, and longed for nothing so much as bed, but she knew that if she didn't assemble her chaotic thoughts into some sort of order and get them down in writing they would be lost. She stifled a yawn, then looked out of the window, across the wild sea—and had the idea. What a superb, what an absolutely magnificent book it would all make! She sat upright, jerked to attention with the sheer power of the thought. Not a novel, but a straightforward setting down of talks with the islanders, in the form of interviews. It had been done before, with various isolated communities, and she had read several, and there was a fascination about hearing of people's thoughts, and ideas, and lives, especially if the compiler of the book knew what he or she was about.

The pattern of their lives would emerge, painted against the sombre, rugged background of a unique island that was possibly like nowhere else on earth. Lory picked up her writing-pad. She had intended writing to her father. She would do so now, while the idea was still fresh, and tell him about it. She valued his opinion highly. And it would still be covered within the scope of her actual work.

She began to write, and silence, save for the slight rustle of paper and the distant thunder of the sea, filled the room. She could hardly believe, even as she wrote, that she had only been on Creagdubh for one full day. Had she really ever imagined it would be dull there? Reading the dry reports, and statistics, it had seemed so. But statistics are not the same as living, breathing people. She visualized the book even as she put the words down to tell her father of it. She couldn't wait to begin . . .

She awoke with a start to find herself still seated at the table, with head down. Blinking, she looked at her watch. Nearly eleven. She had been out for an hour. If that wasn't a signal to go to bed, she didn't know what was. She'd do the notes in the morning. She put the notepad to one side, and went to wash.

Fifteen minutes later she was tucked up in bed, fast asleep.

She breakfasted with Edna and Joan the next morning, and wondered at the subdued atmosphere that filled the place.

Everywhere seemed very silent, even the guests quietly spoken, and she asked them why.

'It's Sunday,' explained Edna. 'You don't know what it's like on Sunday here, do you, dear?' Her sunny round face took on an appropriately solemn expression.

'Of course!' said Lory. 'But I thought—here——' she stopped.

'Oh well,' Joan put in, 'we're used to it—rather like it, in fact—it's very nice to be able to lounge about and take things easy without feeling guilty about it.' And she laughed.

'We didn't see much of you yesterday,' Edna went on. 'Did you have a pleasant day with Mr. Mackinnon?' No doubt Elspeth had told them something, and Lory wondered precisely what.

'Oh yes,' she answered. 'You see, I'm very interested in island life, and it's really part of my job, and he offered to take me round.' She didn't miss the quick glance between the two sisters. They were bound to be curious, not only about her sudden departure the previous day with their host, but also about her changed appearance. The granny glasses had been despatched to the bottom of her case to be returned safely to Kate, her actress friend, at the first possible opportunity. And Lory's hair was now as it had always been, before her stupid attempt at disguise, so that her appearance had been dramatically altered. She smiled at them. They were both genuinely helpful and pleasant, but she didn't want to talk about her work. In a way, it was private, something between her and her reluctant guide and host.

'So you won't be coming with us to see the birds?' asked Joan.

'Er—no, well, not just yet, if you don't mind. As a matter of fact, Mr. Mackinnon took me to a little island yesterday and we saw hundreds of different kinds——' Lory went on to tell them of the various birds, and they listened fascinated, but also, she felt sure, faintly bewildered. She could almost see the questions forming in their minds, questions they would be too polite to ask. It was almost, she realized, as though she were living on a different level. They had been here before, more than once, and yet Lory was certain that they had never really spoken to any islanders. One more thing she realized. If no one went anywhere or did anything on Sundays, she would be able to stay in her room and write up all her notes. She had slept soundly and felt thoroughly refreshed, blisters sore but hardly bothering her, shoulders aching, but so slightly that she was barely conscious of any discomfort.

And when the two men arrived belatedly, she was able to escape. In her room, Lory fetched out her briefcase, then set out the table by the window with all her papers, so that it was like a miniature office, everything neatly laid out to hand. And before she did any writing she was going to read all the reports, especially the nurse's.

Her bed had been made, presumably by Elspeth, and she put her father's letter, which she had almost forgotten about and left on the table all night, on to the bed to finish off later. Then she sat down to read the notes. She saved the nurse's report until last. She wasn't really sure why, except that there had been something disturbing about it before and she wanted a balanced view of everything before beginning her own writing. It was all there on paper, statistics and figures, dry and precise. Population in 1865, types of houses, occupations—population in later years, at twenty-year intervals—all as brisk and impersonal as a graph on an office wall. Exact, but telling nothing of the personalities, of the hearts that dwelt in those houses ... Lory put them aside with a sign of relief. She didn't doubt that they had all been written by men who had not been within a hundred miles of Creagdubh, or any Hebridean island for that matter.

Then she read the last report. There was a difference this time. Before, she had been in London. Now she was here, actually in the place, and had seen it for herself. And she knew, even before she finished the first page of the neatly typed piece, that what she was reading was not strictly accurate. There was nothing flagrantly untrue about it, nothing she could put her finger on and say: but that's ridiculous! It was far more subtle than that. The ex-nurse gave the impression that the islanders were undernourished, of below average intelligence, hostile and suspicious. She put it down half read, and looked away out of the window. Finlay now, one of her first encounters with an islander. What had been her impression, after the first ten minutes' conversation? That here was a shrewd brain. And while he lived in a rather spartan house, he seemed not to lack material comforts—warmth, books, a radio—and he was certainly not undernourished. Anything but! She smiled slowly at the thought. He looked like a man who enjoyed his food to the full.

And then Jean and her children. All bright-eyed and alert, noisy but not badly behaved, merely boisterous. Mr. and Mrs. Campbell were a different matter, but the exile there was self-imposed, and once music had been mentioned any hostility, imagined or otherwise, had vanished. Lory sighed and picked up the paper again. Of course it was possible that everyone else on Creagdubh fitted perfectly the picture the ex-nurse had painted. Possible—but highly improbable. She knew one thing. The sooner she spoke to the present nurse, Sister Grant, the better. Today if possible. Lory looked at her watch. It was nearly eleven. There was no harm in walking along, if only to post her father's letter at the post office. No one could object to that, surely? And if by chance she called at the nurse's on the way back...

It was decided. She would go after lunch. When she had returned to the house the previous evening, Grant had said nothing about today, merely that he would probably see her at breakfast. But he had not appeared. Elspeth, helped by a girl from the village, had served them, and then vanished. All was quiet. Her bed was made, so there would be no interruption. Lory, after a final look round the table, set to work writing her notes.

Even the lunch gong had a muted tone to it, as if in deference to the Sabbath. Lory sighed with relief, rubbed her aching wrist, and pushed away the paper she had been writing on. She felt satisfied with her morning's work—and ready for a good walk after lunch. Quickly she put everything into the briefcase, locked it in the wardrobe, finished and sealed her father's letter, and went down to her meal.

She sat with Edna and Joan, while Ellis and Raymond were at a nearby table with two other men. There seemed to be no rule as to who sat where, in fact the atmosphere of the place was completely informal. And yet, today, there was something not quite right. The two sisters were pleasant enough; it certainly was not that. And then, as Elspeth brought in the sweet, the back of Lory's neck prickled, and she knew what was wrong. The previous day, when she had been in the kitchen, she had sensed the housekeeper's faint disapproval. It was no longer that; it was hostility, veiled, subtle, probably not apparent to Lory's two companions, but there all the same.

She smiled at Elspeth as she put the sponge pudding before her. 'Thank you,' she said. And Elspeth turned away, not too quickly, but Lory knew quite clearly. It was not her imagination. She felt a sense of dismay, trying to rationalize the feeling. It was human enough not to want to be disliked, Lory knew that well. But she hadn't imagined she would feel *hurt* by the woman's attitude. Edna and Joan chattered away happily, and she made the right responses in the right places, and wondered what was happening to her that she should be so bothered by something so unimportant. Or was it? Was it by some means connected with Grant Mackinnon? There was no way to answer that, only wait and see.

She told the sisters that she was walking to the village to post a letter when lunch was finished, and had they anything they needed posting? They had, and Lory waited in that dark beautiful panelled hall while they went up to their room. All was quiet, save for the ticking of the grandfather clock in a corner near the stairs. Once there was a sound from the kitchen, and a door closing, then faint voices, but that was all. She might have been alone.

Then women's voices, descending, and the two sisters appeared, and handed her a letter each which she put in her bag with her father's, said her farewells, and went out of the front door. The fresh wind soon chased away any cobwebs of depressing thoughts, and Lory's natural cheerfulness asserted itself again as she walked at a brisk pace down the drive, and towards the gate. There was nothing she could do about Elspeth, so she didn't intend to waste time brooding on the matter.

The sombre beauty of Creagdubh was already exerting a subtle influence on Lory; she knew that, and was faintly surprised at it, for didn't she love London more than any place she had ever known? Yet still, as she walked that narrow road, she sensed the pull of the place, almost a tangible thing. It did not welcome you, as a warm seaside resort did, it did not proclaim its attractions blatantly, but it was there all the same, and she felt a tugging at her heart strings at the sheer bleak ruggedness of it all. It seemed to be saying: take me as I am, here nothing is easy, but the rewards are endless. She mentally shrugged. I'm getting sentimental and fanciful in my old age, she thought, and glanced round her, wondering why it should be so. And the image of Grant Mackinnon's face was there, as if he *was* Creagdubh. She knew why, suddenly. He was part of the island, he was at one with it, at home, as tough and rugged as the very contours of the island, as bleakly uncompromising in his very being. And she recalled how he had been at the Campbells'—a different man when he had spoken to that pale grey woman. Different too with Finlay—and with Jean and her children. A complex man, and one of her first impressions of him came back to tease her as she walked quickly along. She had seen him as a man who would fight the world for what he thought was right—and never yield.

A little shiver touched her spine. How frightened she had been on their first stormy encounter on the road back from the village on the Friday evening! She had thought he intended pushing her over the cliff—absurd to think of it in the cold clear light of day—and yet not absurd *then*, when they had been alone, and his mood had been one of hard sparking anger. Lory sighed. All in all, he was quite a man. 'The understatement of the year,' she said softly, out loud, and the wind whipped the spoken thought away to vanish instantly.

Nearly there now. She could see the houses in the distance, a grey huddle, and beyond them the waters of the loch, whisked to white horses by the wind, stronger there. Behind that the dark hills. And all was silent. She had passed the nurse's house, and the school, and seen no one at either. She wondered what people did all day on a Sunday. There would be no Sunday papers to read, Edna had already told her that. If any came at all, it was on Monday, with the plane, or a boat from the mainland. Lory felt almost obliged to tiptoe past those first houses, and had to resist the impulse strongly. But she walked more slowly, quietly, and almost jumped when a dog barked from the distance, so unexpected was the sound.

The letterbox was there, set in the post office wall, proudly proclaiming 'V.R.' in ornate letters. She looked briefly at the telephone box before checking that the three letters were all sealed and stamped and posting them. Her father would love a call from her, but what would the operator think? It would be unimaginable for anyone to call anywhere on the Sabbath, save in dire emergency. And where would they telephone then? It was the only phone for miles and miles. The thought was almost frightening, bringing home sharply to Lory just how used she was to services of all kinds at hand, within a few minutes, just by picking up a receiver and dialling. Here everyone depended on their neighbours, or themselves. And perhaps, above all, they depended on Grant. Fish to the people, blankets for Jean's family, roof mending for the Campbells.

And what more? She looked briefly in the post office window, crammed with every imaginable kind of commodity from tinned food to fishing tackle, tins of talcum powder and plastic mackintoshes and socks and rolls of film and a paraffin lamp and a cat. A cat! She looked more closely and it stirred and opened one eye, then closed it again. She could almost hear it purr, and so it should, curled up on a pile of scarves as it was. Smiling, Lory turned away. She wondered if they sold picture postcards. Taking a deep breath, she set off towards home—but before that, a visit to the nurse.

CHAPTER SEVEN

LORY was passing the schoolhouse when she heard a faint shout, and looked around. Mrs. Macleod stood in the doorway beckoning her. Smiling, she went up the path, towards the beaming schoolmistress.

'We saw you pass before,' she whispered, almost pulling Lory into the living room, 'come away in. It's not really done to visit on the Sabbath, but I don't think anyone saw you.'

'I don't think so,' Lory grinned. 'I felt quite guilty coming to post, but I needed the walk.'

'Aye well, sit down. You'll have a cup of tea?'

'I'd love one.'

'And I've looked out that book for you. I said to my Donald you'd no doubt be coming this way again before long. Well now, how do you like Creagdubh?'

'I like it very much,' said Lory truthfully, settling herself in a comfortable chair where she was immediately joined by the cat. She smiled at the older woman, whose pleasant face showed keen interest, genuine, she felt sure.

'Good, good. I'll away and make the tea. Donald is just now having a bath, but he will be down in a minute or two. And then we can have a nice chat.' She vanished into the kitchen and Lory relaxed and stroked the cat, staring at the fire in the grate, enjoying the comfort after her walk, blithely unaware of the shock to come.

'Ach now, ye'll have a wee scone as well. That's it, just help yourself, there are plenty more.' Mrs. Macleod seated herself comfortably, wedging her ample body into the matching easy chair, and picking up her cup. 'You did not tell

99

us you were a sociologist.'

It sank in slowly, for Lory was in the middle of biting into a delicious scone when she said it. Then: 'Oh! You know!'

'My dear,' Mrs. Macleod smiled wryly, 'it does not take five minutes for news to travel in this place. You are the sole topic of conversation at the moment. Creagdubh has never had a sociologist before, indeed and I'm not sure if half of them know what it means.'

She should have known. She really should have. She looked the friendly woman in the eye. 'I tried—foolishly—to keep it secret when I came, in case anyone misunderstood my motives, but Grant forced it out of me.'

Mrs. Macleod chuckled. 'He did now? Well, I could have warned you had I known. He's a sharp one, he is, make no mistake.'

'Yes, I know that now,' agreed Lory dryly. 'You'd have thought I was here to murder everyone, the way he went on——' She stopped, suddenly aware that she was probably saying too much. But Mrs. Macleod was equally shrewd, and smiled gently.

'It's all right, lass,' she said quietly. 'You don't need to worry, with us. I'm the schoolteacher. I cannot afford to go exchanging gossip with the islanders. I know fine well what Grant Mackinnon is like. I know why you're here too. Or I can imagine well. And you said something on your last visit to us of a report done by our ex-nurse, did you not?'

'Yes.' Lory looked at her. There was something behind the other's words ... 'I was hoping to call in on Sister Grant this afternoon, just to get one or two points cleared up. Do you think she'd mind?'

'Ach, she's like us. She'd be delighted. She keeps in on the Sabbath, so as not to offend the islanders, unless anyone is ill, of course, but she is not one of them any more than we are. You go along there, and have your chat. But there's one thing, of course—she never was here when the other nurse —Sister Monroe—was working here, so she doesn't know——' It was her turn to stop now.

Lory felt as if she was standing on a cliff edge. Every move had to be delicate, well considered, before it was made. 'She doesn't know what, Mrs. Macleod?' she asked very gently.

'Why, the truth, of course. The truth of why she left. You told us about this report, and Donald and I talked it over since, and we can imagine the kind of things it would say, because we knew her. We probably knew her better than most people here, us being neighbours, and in a similar way of business—if you know what I mean?'

Lory nodded. Her mouth had gone quite dry. 'Yes, I know,' she said. 'But what do you mean by the truth?'

'The real reason why she left, why she became so bitter—and why, I shouldn't be surprised, she vowed she would get even with Grant Mackinnon. Can you not imagine what it was?'

Lory could, but before she committed herself to any rash statements she had to ask something. 'Was Sister Monroe young?' she said.

'Oh aye, late twenties, I'd say—and a fine-looking girl too. Only she made the mistake of 'falling in love with Grant Mackinnon.'

So much became clearer, sharply focussed, instead of blurred and incomplete, as it had been. Lory was still shaken when she left the Macleods' a short time later, clutching the book she had borrowed, promising to return it safely when she visited them again. Of course! Everything fell into place. The jarring inconsistencies of Sister Monroe's report were to be seen in a new light now. All because of an explanation that probably no one else could—or would—have given her. She walked away from the schoolhouse quickly, her head reeling with what she had been told. And the rest—the words unspoken, the glances between Mr. and Mrs. Macleod, told even more. Grant Mackinnon was not interested in women, they seemed to say. He was, in particular, not interested in the nurse. And he had made it only too clear.

Lory shivered, for it had gone colder, or was it just her? She didn't know. For she was remembering Grant's own reaction at her mention of the nurse, the sudden upsurge of anger, the way he had held the stone as if he might crush it. That there was more than even the Macleods knew, she did not doubt. But one thing was certain: he wouldn't tell her. She slowed her footsteps as she neared Sister Grant's cottage. She didn't really want to go there, not just now, she had too much to think about. But she had told the Macleods she would, and they might mention it. Reluctantly she opened the little gate and walked up the path towards the door. She might not answer, she might be resting, or not hear ...

'Hello, come on in.' The door had opened so quietly that as Lory looked up, she was there, standing in the porch, a good-looking woman of about forty-five, dark-haired, with a nice smile and friendly eyes. 'You'll be Miss Stevenson, our sociologist, will you?'

'Yes—how did you——' Lory began, and then started laughing. 'Oh, don't tell me, let me guess. I'm the——'

'Sole topic of conversation hereabouts,' the nurse finished for her, joining in her laughter. 'That's about it. Come on in, then, it'll be nice to talk to someone from civilization.'

What a welcome there was in the house! It was simply furnished, but warm, and Sister Grant had plants everywhere—everywhere, that is, that was not taken up with books. Lory sighed appreciatively. 'You're a reader too,' she said.

'I am. Sit you down. Coffee?'

'Well—I've just had tea at the schoolhouse, but you go ahead.'

'Oh no, it can wait.' Sister Grant closed a book she had clearly been reading, and added: 'Well, go on. Fire away.'

Lory grinned. They were on the same wavelength, that was clear. 'Would you believe this is more or less a social call?' she asked.

'If you say so. But I'm disappointed. I had visions of being interviewed, asked for my opinions. However——' she shrugged. 'Not to worry. I always like a chat about anything. What's it to be? Books? Theatre? Films?'

Lory laughed. 'Don't you find it very quiet here after Edinburgh?'

'I do. But not too much so. It takes hold of you after a while, you know, although you'll hardly have had time yet to know what I mean——' But I do, thought Lory, I do. 'And as long as I go back to Auld Reekie for a holiday now and then, I'm quite happy here with my books. How did you know I came from Edinburgh anyway?'

'Oh well, I've got papers and reports,' answered Lory. 'One of which told me all about Sister Grant and how efficient she is.'

'Oh, good. Nice to know I'm appreciated. And the name's Betty. I get a bit sick of the Sister Grant bit sometimes, you know.'

'And mine's Lory. And I will have that coffee now, if I may.'

'Right you are. Two coffees coming up!'

Betty Grant knew London well, and had travelled widely. She was a widow with two grown-up children, both married and living in Edinburgh, and she had three grandchildren who were coming over for a visit in a few weeks. The time sped by so quickly that it was with a sense of shock that Lory heard the clock strike five.

'Good grief!' she exclaimed. 'Is *that* the time?'

'You're not worried?' Betty Grant said. 'Have you to be back?'

'No. Dinner's not till seven, but it's nearly an hour's walk—I didn't realize we'd been talking so long.'

'Aye, it's gone quickly all right. You must come again soon, Lory. I've enjoyed this.'

'So have I. You've given me a lot to think about.'

Betty Grant smiled. 'Have I now? That's interesting.

Well, I hope I've been of help, that's all. Now don't forget, come back any time. I'm not busy here all the time, and you can browse among my books, and borrow what you want.'

'Thanks, I'll remember that. And thanks for the coffee.'

The wind had risen, and Lory set off once again, and this time her head was whirling with information. If there was a book to be written about the island, Betty Grant could well do it herself, even though she had been there only a short time. She was clearly a shrewd observer of life. Her words came back to Lory as she strode along, leaning into the wind.

'Of course,' she had said, at one point in their conversation, as they both sat drinking their coffee, 'they never really accept you as one of them unless you're born here. Oh, they're polite and courteous, but it's also a terribly proud, close-knit community. They accept me as their nurse, but I'm aware that I'm a stranger, and will remain so until I go. On the other hand there is a childish honesty to them that is appealing. There is no greed here, it's share and share alike. It has a lot to recommend it, a community like this has. They're all healthy enough, though we have the odd hypochondriac—but you get that anywhere. One dear old lady swears she would die without her little red pills three times a day, but I, and Sister Monroe, and her predecessor before her, all keep a secret. Her little red pills are placebos—sugar and colouring, and have been for years. But they keep her going. To her, they're nothing short of a magic potion. They're quite superstitious—but aren't all small communities, to a certain extent?' She had picked up Lory's borrowed book then. 'Yet they wouldn't tell me anything, of course. No one's ever mentioned seeing the Moon-dancers to me, because I'm an outsider.'

'But then how come,' Lory had asked, 'did they talk to you about *me*?' It was a logical enough question, and Betty had laughed.

'But you're an outsider too, don't you see?'

An outsider. The words lingered in Lory's mind as she

walked slowly along. Of course she was. And if she stayed here for ever, she still would be—and wasn't that an absurd thought to have! She had no intention of staying longer than three weeks, and then she'd be away, back home to London, and it would be goodbye, Finlay, and Jean, and everyone. And goodbye, Grant. She would never see him again. And suddenly Lory knew something deep inside her, in the very core of her being. She would never see him again, but she would never forget him.

There was just time to make notes on her afternoon's conversations when she reached her room, and wash before dinner. She had not changed the previous night, but most of the others had, and it had been pleasant to see long dresses worn by Edna and Joan and a few of the other women. Lory went to her wardrobe. She had brought a floor-length evening skirt with her, and three blouses. The skirt was of dark green and blue wool, softly shaded, slim-fitting and elegant, one of her favourites which had the added advantage of travelling well. She took it out now and looked at it. Why not? she thought. Her frumpy image was gone for good. And she needed, suddenly, to feel as if she *looked* good—which she knew she did when she wore the skirt. She rifled through her wardrobe until she found the blouse she liked best, a blue courtelle which matched the blue of the skirt to perfection. It took only a minute or so to dress, to smooth the skirt over her slim hips, to zip it up—and she looked in the mirror. I might as well go the whole hog, she thought, sat down at her dressing table, and began to make up.

But she wasn't prepared to see Grant as she went down the stairs. She caught her breath as she saw him crossing the hall, and he stopped, and looked up at her, and she saw first the surprise in his eyes—then a reflection of what she had seen in Elspeth's—blank, shuttered hostility.

'Good evening,' she said.

'Good evening.' He barely nodded. As she reached him,

105

she went on:

'May I visit the library after dinner?'

'If you wish.' The contrast from yesterday was startling. The dark blue eyes surveyed her with cool indifference. She wanted to ask: What is it? What's the matter? but she could not. There was a barrier between them that she feared to touch. Her heart beat faster—and then he turned and walked away, quite simply walked away and left her standing there feeling foolish. She felt the anger rising in her, and suppressed it. It would do no good—yet she wanted to run after him, to swing him round, to *shake* him—to say——

Footsteps descending the stairs, voices, more of the guests coming down for dinner. Lory turned and walked, head held high, into the dining room. There were several others there, and she felt the ripple of admiration as she entered. This was what she was used to, this, not being ignored. She smiled and said her hellos, and went and sat down. But it had all gone sour. It just didn't mean anything any more. The only thing that mattered was a hard-eyed, hostile man who wore old clothes and walked with an air that said he didn't give a damn for her. One of the men came over to talk, a middle-aged solicitor from Wakefield who had a shy pleasant smile and manner.

She didn't even remember afterwards what they had spoken about, except that she had smiled a lot, and laughed at his pleasantries, in case *he* was watching, so that he would know she didn't care at all for *his* opinion. It was a wasted effort, because Grant never appeared at all, and Elspeth and the girl from the village, Catriona who was no more than seventeen, served them with dinner. Lory had no appetite, and Edna remarked on it, enquiring if she felt poorly.

'A slight headache,' Lory answered with some truth. 'But it'll go away.' The women insisted she have two aspirins with her coffee and said they were going out for a walk, would she like to come? So she told them that she was going to get a book from the library and would probably take it to her room to read there, which they, with much nodding, said was a good idea. 'It's the air, you see, dear,' explained Edna kindly, 'it's such a complete change here. A quiet evening will do you good.'

Lory wondered about that when she eventually left them and went to the large room at the back of the house. She was not sure if a quiet evening was what she needed after all, for she felt strangely restless and ill at ease, and there was nothing she could do about it.

There were thousands of books, row upon row, stretching from floor to ceiling, and several easy chairs in the vast room in which she found herself. And it was so quiet with the dry air, faintly dusty, that is usually to be found in libraries. She closed the door and began to look around, bewildered with the selection, unsure of where to begin, even forgetting the smouldering anger that still lay beneath the surface because Grant had rudely walked away and left her...

'Well, have you found anything?' his deep voice came from the doorway, and then he walked in and closed the door quietly behind him, and stood there watching her.

I must be calm, she thought. Calm and cool. I must not get angry. I must *not*. 'Not yet,' and she smiled. 'But I've only been here a few minutes and the choice is overwhelming.'

'Yes, it is.' He walked towards her.

'You can leave me to browse,' she said sweetly. 'I promise I won't steal any.'

'I didn't imagine you would.' His voice was harsh. 'And I'm not staying. I just came to say that I will take you to Jean's tomorrow. That is if you want to go—and you do want to *talk* to people, do you not?'

No doubt about the hard edge to his voice, nor the smile on his face—not a pleasant smile, but as hard as his voice.

'That would be nice. Thank you.' She inclined her head graciously, quite in command of the situation, not *at all* bothered by him . . .

'Good. About nine-thirty? The children will be at school then. You will really be able to have a pleasant chat, will you not?'

'Indeed yes.' She half turned away as if to dismiss him. The trouble was, she realized a moment later, he didn't dismiss so easily. He moved nearer to her, folding his arms and leaning nonchalantly against his books.

'Is there anything else?' she asked. Her temper was fraying rapidly, all her firm resolves slipping and melting away in the brittle tension that seemed, suddenly, to be filling the room.

'Anything else?' he mused over the words. '*Is* there anything else?'

'I'm asking *you*,' she snapped, resisting the urge to throw a book—any book—at him.

'Ach, no. I was just looking at your—outfit.' He made it sound faintly insulting. 'You look—different tonight. Is there any reason?'

'Should there be?' He hadn't said she looked nice, and that rankled.

'Why, no. It is pleasant to see a woman in a long dress. Old-fashioned—suitable.'

Lory looked him up and down, very slowly. 'It would be nice to see a man who took the trouble to dress for dinner as well,' she remarked, fighting hard to hold to the last fragments of her composure.

'Ach, I am but a poor Scotsman,' Grant said mockingly, 'what would I be doing in fancy clothes?'

'I'm sure I don't know,' she said tartly. 'Why don't you just go and leave me *alone*?'

He drew in his breath sharply, as if she had drawn blood. 'It is my house,' he said quietly. 'Or had you forgotten?'

'I don't think I could ever forget that fact,' she answered. 'Or that it is *your* island either. Is that what you want me to say?'

A muscle moved in his jaw. 'Perhaps it will have to do,

for a start,' he rejoined smoothly. 'Gradually you will learn. You will learn.'

Lory stood very still. Very, very still. This was no ordinary conversation. It had gone beyond that. She felt as if she were standing on a quicksand, as if the slightest wrong move would bring disaster upon her—yet she did not know which way to turn for safety.

'What will I learn?' she asked quietly.

'That this island is as it always was—and always will be. You will not change it. Nothing you can do will accomplish that. I do not care where you are from, or why. Creagdubh is greater than both of us, but I am for it, and you—what are you? You are the stranger who has come to try and see what you can do—but you will not change anything. I promise you that.'

'I don't know what you mean,' she said faintly.

'Do you not? Then think about it. Ponder on it when you go to bed tonight, and hear the sea dashing against the rocks, and the wind whistling round the walls of this house, and know that you are nothing. Absolutely nothing.' And he turned and walked away from her and went out of the door, and it closed quietly behind him, and Lory was left alone.

Slowly, shuddering, she went to the table and sat down before her legs gave way beneath her. She knew there was something at the back of her mind. Something that would supply the answer to all his cryptic remarks—but for the life of her, at that moment, she could not think what it was. She looked down at her hands on the table. Tomorrow, tomorrow, she had a feeling she would find out.

'Oh, do sit down,' said Jean. 'Now we can talk,' and she beamed at Lory. 'There is only wee Donald at home now,' and she picked him up and hugged him. 'But he's a good boy, aren't you, love? Now where are your cars? Get them from the cupboard and have a nice game.' She winked at Lory. They were sitting in the comfortable, untidy living room of Jean's house, and Grant had left her there some minutes previously after a strangely silent journey from Creagdubh House. She wondered where he had gone, but hadn't dared to ask. He had not even come up to the house with her, but left her at the foot of the track, and driven off.

'You missed Iain, my husband, again. He went off early this morning, just as Grant arrived——' and then she stopped, slightly confused, it seemed to Lory's acute eyes.

'Grant? But he just brought me now,' she exclaimed.

'Aye well, he came before, early, as I was making breakfast.' She looked at Lory, and bit her lip, her face a mixture of embarrassment and dismay. 'I'll just make us a cup of tea,' and she turned away to the fire where the kettle bubbled noisily. Lory looked at Donald sitting happily on the floor with several little cars which he pushed briskly about with much 'brumm-brumming.'

Jean was very busy, it seemed, with making tea, and getting beakers and milk, and a basin of sugar, and she did not meet Lory's eyes until she sat down, and then said: 'Well, it's no use, is it? I can't sit here and talk to you all morning, and pretend nothing's amiss. I like you, and I trust you, and while Grant is an old and dear friend, I do not always agree with everything he does, and that's a fact.'

'I'm not sure if I understand,' said Lory slowly, which was also a fact, but at the same time, instinct told her that the previous evening's disturbing conversation in the library might be about to be explained. 'But please don't feel you have to tell me anything, if you don't want to.'

'Ach, I'm not supposed to, but men! Sometimes they can be very exasperating—they think they are the lords of creation, yet where would they be without us? They're as helpless as babies most of the time, for all they think they're tough.' She laughed. 'I love my Iain dearly, but he and Grant are like two brothers, as close as that. I dare say it's because they were at school together as wee lads. And as far as Iain is concerned, whatever Grant says is perfect, and that's that. But I've a mind of my own, thank the Lord, so

I'll tell you what it is that has got Grant so mad.'

'Go on,' prompted Lory softly. Her instinct had been right.

'Well, he told us this morning that you are planning to write a book about us, the islanders, and pry into all our secrets——' She stopped at seeing Lory's shocked face. 'Are you all right?'

'Yes. Please go on.'

'And that's about it. Except that he says it will be over his dead body. I have never seen him so angry. That's why he brought you here first. So that he could warn everyone——' Lory felt sick. Not only at Jean's words, which were shocking enough, but at the realization that there was only one way Grant could have found out. Her letter to her father. He must have read it, actually *read* a private letter which she had been stupid enough to leave lying about.

'Drink your tea, Lory. I'm sorry. Have I upset you?' Jean was genuinely concerned, and Lory, knowing her condition, knowing she must not say anything to distress this kindly woman, shook her head.

'Heavens, no,' she laughed—with an effort. 'But I'm pleased you told me. I was awfully puzzled by his behaviour last night, and this morning. Now you've explained it. I can understand. He's got it all wrong. I wouldn't be prying, or anything like that, just writing down people's views on life here in Creagdubh, describing the island—you know the kind of thing.' She shrugged. 'However, if he feels as strongly as that about it, I'll have to shelve the idea, won't I?' She smiled reassuringly at Jean. 'And don't worry, Jean. I will not, of course, say a word about you to him. You have my promise on that.'

'I'm glad. I knew I could trust you. And you understand why I couldn't keep silent about it? I'd feel like a traitor, keeping you here talking—out of the way, as it were. Anyway, I think it's a good idea. It's about time someone wrote a book about us, put us on the map, as you might say!' She chuckled.

'Ach, never mind. I know what he means, in a way I suppose. He's like a mother hen with her chicks, is our bonny laird. Fiercely protective. I could tell you about some of the things he's done, that I'm not supposed to know about—but I dare not. But I can tell you this. He's changed this island for the better since his great-uncle died, and he took over. He works hard, and it's not for himself, it's for others. Everyone here loves him—and I'm not putting it too strongly at that—and they'd do anything for him, which is why, if he tells them all not to tell you *anything*, then they won't.'

Lory put her hand to her forehead. 'Oh, Jean,' she said, 'what am I to do?' She looked up, anguished. 'I came here with such high ideals—such plans. I feel as if I might as well just go. I know that what you say is true. I've been to the Campbells' with him, while he mended their roof—I've heard the way he talks to poor Mrs. Campbell—and it wasn't put on for my benefit, he's kind and gentle with her, and she responds to him.'

'Aye, she does. I've spoken to her husband, when he's come to the village, and he says the same. And Finlay now—you've met him, of course. Grant takes Finlay out fishing nearly every week. The old man lives for that, he does. Says he can almost see the fish—but I'm talking too much, am I not? And I said I wouldn't.'

'It doesn't matter now,' said Lory softly. 'I won't be writing any of it down, I assure you. The only notes I make will be strictly impersonal ones—like the kind I've been reading in some reports. Just facts and figures about the number of people living here, age groups—that sort of thing. I've spoken to Sister Grant as well, and it seems as if Creagdubh is a healthy place, taking it all round——'

'Och, it is! With this air!' Jean laughed. 'The only trouble is, so few young people, but that's a problem we share with many other isolated communities, and there's not much anyone can do about *that.*'

'No, I know. If only the nurse's report hadn't been so

112

definite that all was not well——'

'The nurse? You mean Sister Grant—or the other one?'
There was something odd about Jean's voice.

'Not Sister Grant. I mean Sister Monroe.'

'Ach, *her*!' The contempt on Jean's face was sudden and
startling. 'You read something *she* had written?' And she
looked across at her son, innocently and happily playing on
the rug.

'Yes. It was she who started it all, in a way. But now,
since I've spoke to—er—one or two—I realize that what
she said wasn't strictly accurate——'

'Accurate!' Jean looked at Lory, and her eyes were lit
with scorn. 'You should have asked me about her, Lory. I
would have told you. She was not fit to be called a nurse,
that one. We are well rid of her!'

'I don't think you'd better tell me any more, Jean,' said
Lory quietly. 'It's over and done now, whatever it was—
and I have a good idea——'

'Do you? No, I don't think you do. Och, I can guess
what you've heard—that she fell for Grant, yes—is that
it?'

'Something like that,' Lory admitted. She was more concerned about Jean getting upset than talking about Grant.

'Aye, well, I know the truth of that. And there's very few
who do, believe me—whatever you've heard. Oh, Lory,' she
got up abruptly, and went to the teapot in the hearth, 'let's
have another cup. I cannot even think about that one without getting cross. A cup of tea will do me good!' And she
managed a smile, much to Lory's relief.

When she was seated again, after giving her son a cup of
milk and a biscuit, Jean said: 'I'll tell you briefly, just this
once. But after that I'll never speak of her again.' She
patted her stomach. 'I'm just so glad that it's Sister Grant
who will deliver this one, believe me.' She sipped her tea,
and Lory, bemused, did the same. It was strong from
standing—but she felt as if she needed it.

'I sensed she was trouble the day she came. Och, it was

113

nothing you could put your finger on exactly, but it was there—a sort of patronizing attitude, the kind that gets your back up, and we canna' have strangers coming here and thinking they're better than us. Grant wasn't back here then, for his uncle was still alive—old Mackinnon, that was—so you could say there were no young men—no single ones, that is.' And here she paused, and Lory guessed what was to come. 'It didn't take me five minutes to see she was after my Iain. She was always asking him to go and do little jobs at her house—the roof was leaking, the ground was too hard for her to bury her rubbish—that sort of thing.'

She pulled a face. 'She must have thought I was a daftie! The cheeky madam! Iain didn't have much choice, for he did jobs for the laird, who was too old to do anything himself, and he is kindness itself, but he told me he didn't want to go there any more one day, so I told him not to go—she'd have to manage herself. And then old Mackinnon died, rest his soul, and Grant returned—and you should have seen her face then! You'd ha' thought it was her birthday! I'll bet she could see herself set up as the laird's wife in no time—and poor Elspeth would have been put out to grass right smart, for if ever two women didn't get on, it was Elspeth and Sister Monroe. Elspeth saw through her right away. But Grant didn't want anything to do with her—until one day, when he was here, and I was feeling pretty low—I was expecting wee Donald then—I told him how she'd been chasing after my Iain, and how upset I was. And he said something like—not to worry—and I didn't understand what he meant, until it appeared that he was becoming interested in her, at which time she completely lost all interest in Iain—for which I was greatly relieved, for even though I trust my man completely, they can still be led by temptation, can they not?'

'I suppose so,' Lory smiled gently. 'You mean that Grant deliberately set out after her? After he'd not been at all interested?'

'I mean that exactly. And now I know why—but I didn't

then. I thought the poor man had gone and fallen for her. I began to feel sorry for him—and for Elspeth!'

'And then what happened?' Lory prompted, quite agog with curiosity despite her previous determination not to know.

'Why, nothing! All of a sudden, the rumours went that she was leaving—and it was so. Sister Grant flew in, and Sister Monroe flew out hours later—and that was that. And it was good riddance to her. Sister Grant now, she's smashing. Just the sort we need here.' She sighed, and put down her empty beaker. 'And that's that. And if that other one has been saying anything about this place I can imagine why. What is that old saying "hell hath no fury——?"?'

' "Like a woman scorned"?' Lory finished for her. 'Yes, I can see it all now. She certainly managed to stir it up all right. Oh dear, oh dear!' She shook her head.

'But you can put things right, can't you?' Jean's face showed her concern.

'To a certain extent, yes. I mean, I can hardly put a report in that everyone can ignore everything Sister Monroe said because she was suffering from an acute case of rejection—but I can say how I've found everything, and that this seems to be a thriving community with few problems—there are such things as government grants for islands like this one, for improvements to houses——'

'But Grant would never accept charity!' Jean cut in, appalled.

'It's not charity! Heavens, what do you think people pay taxes for? It would be what you all are entitled to, and there's a difference.'

'Aye well, I don't know,' Jean looked doubtful. 'But then that's nothing to do with me, thank the Lord. That's something you'll have to sort out for yourself. Now then, what say you we talk about something different—like the games on Saturday?' and she beamed at Lory, clearly having decided that enough had been said on a certain subject.

It was a relief to Lory too. 'The games?' she answered.

'What games—and where? Here?'

'Och no,' Jean laughed. 'Where would we find a field flat enough? We're all hills and mountains! They're on a neighbouring island about ten miles away—ye'll have flown over it on the plane, no doubt, and sure, it's hardly as big as Creagdubh, but it's their main event of the year.'

'Tell me more,' said Lory, fascinated. 'Does everyone go?'

'Everyone that can. I'll be going, with Iain and the bairns, and Sister Grant, and the Macleods—and a lot more you'll not have met yet. We go early on Saturday, and it's late when we return that night, but oh! what a day it will be!'

'It sounds marvellous,' said Lory. 'Is it a real Highland games?'

'Well, I dare say it's a wee bit *smaller* than the Braemar Gathering,' Jean laughed, 'but it's grand enough for us, I can tell you.' She looked pensive. 'Let me see, there's the pipes, of course—and the races, and the hammer throwing and shot putting—and the caber tossing——' then she paused. 'Though mind, I'm not sure if Grant will be going in for that this year at all, but my Iain is.'

The picture conjured up in Lory's mind was so vivid that for a few moments she was wordless. Then she managed: 'But caber tossing? I thought that was always done by twenty-stone giants in kilts!' It was no use trying to keep straight faces—they both began to laugh, Jean until the tears ran down her cheeks.

'Och, my, what a thought! Aye well, you're right enough, in one way. I dare say you'll have seen some on television? Twenty-stone giants! Oh, deary me,' and she wiped her cheek with her fingers. 'I must tell Iain that!'

'Oh dear!' Lory was dismayed. 'I didn't mean——'

'I know fine what you meant! Och, Iain is big—like Grant, in fact they're much of a size—but it's strength and skill that count, and they've both got that. You'll see for yourself anyway. You'll be going with us, of course?' She was still greatly amused, not one whit offended, and clearly looking forward to telling her husband of Lory's remarks.

'Well——' began Lory. 'I'd love to—but if Grant is being—well, you know—he might not want me to go.'

'Och, never mind him! You'll come with us anyway. That's if you'd like to—as long as you don't mind keeping an eye on the bairns with me.'

'I'd like that.' It seemed to be settled. Jean had a remarkable way of making things sound so simple.

And then, before they could say any more, they heard footsteps crunching up the path, and a knock came at the door. It was Grant.

'Hello, Grant,' Jean called. 'Come away in and have a cup of tea. I was just now telling Lory of the games, and inviting her to come with us.' And with a wink at Lory, she carried the teapot over to the kettle.

Lory looked up at him towering in the open doorway, and their eyes met in a silent, startling challenge. This was the man who had dared to read her letter, whose hostility was barely concealed, who didn't want her there *at all*. So what would he say to *that*?

He came in and closed the door behind him. 'That will be fine,' he said quietly. 'Just fine. I'm sure you'll enjoy yourself—Lory.'

CHAPTER EIGHT

A MAN of constant surprises; of ever-changing moods. Lory watched him drinking his tea, and that thought came to her. He bent to pick up a car of Donald's, to admire it, and the little boy looked up at him, eyes shining with laughter as Grant spoke softly to him. Over their heads, Jean nodded briefly to Lory, as if to say: See, I told you it would be all right, and Lory smiled in silent reply.

But then they left a few minutes later, he was different again. Hard-voiced, hard-eyed. 'I'm away to do a job nearby the Campbells',' he said. 'You'll come with me?' It wasn't really a question. He wasn't asking, he was telling her.

'Oh, yes. Fine.' She kept her voice deliberately cool. She had given her word to Jean, and could not say what she knew about his reading the letter, but the brittle tension was there all right, and she didn't care if it was obvious. She was bursting inside to let him know what she thought of him, and she had to suppress her feelings. How she longed to let rip, but it was impossible. Yet something of it must have communicated itself to him, for as they drove past the village he glanced at her.

'Do you never relax?' he said.

'What do you mean?'

'Look at you, sitting there all tensed up. You'll have an ulcer before you're much older if you carry on like that.'

'There's nothing wrong with me,' she snapped. 'And if I'm sitting like this it's because of the way you're driving.'

'Och, is that a fact?' His voice was as mocking as his face. 'Ye'll have to get used to rough roads while you're

118

here, for there's nothing to be done about them. You would perhaps prefer to be chauffeured around in a Rolls-Royce, then?'

'Don't be silly,' she retorted. 'If you went a bit slower you'd do better—and your tyres and springs would probably last a lot longer.'

'Like this?' He slowed down so abruptly that she was nearly jerked out of her seat, and had to put her hands on the dashboard, and brace her feet. 'Is that better?' He was now driving along at something like ten miles an hour, and Lory felt her mouth tighten in helpless anger. 'I didn't realize you were such an expert on vehicles,' he went on, almost amused. 'It must be wonderful to be so clever.'

'It's just common sense, that's all.' She wondered how she was managing to keep from hitting him. Never had a man aroused such primitive rage in her before. Never had anybody been capable, with just a few softly spoken, mocking words, of disturbing her so.

'Och, is it? And you'll have plenty of that, won't you?'

'If you're trying to insult me, you won't succeed. So why don't you save your breath to concentrate on your driving?' she answered.

'Because I want to see what makes you tick, that's why,' he said. 'I want to know what makes you think you can teach us anything.'

'I didn't come here to do that. I came——'

'Och, I know fine why you came. You don't need to tell me. You came here because you thought we were a crowd of simple peasants—only we're not, Miss Lory Stevenson— we're very far from that. And by God, you'll find out before you go home to London!'

His hands gripped the steering wheel tightly so that his knuckles showed white. He's as angry as I am, she thought, and it was sobering. Yet in a way it made her reckless. It was as if she wanted to see how far he would go.

She began to laugh, softly at first—and then jerked into silence as Grant stopped the Range-Rover abruptly. And then she turned to him, fearful of what she might see—and saw the dark anger deep within his eyes—and knew she had her wish.

'Go on, laugh,' he said softly, oh, so softly, and tension throbbed between them like a drumbeat of silent sound. 'And then tell me why you are laughing.'

She couldn't. Her throat had gone tight, as if she might choke, and she could scarcely breathe. She sensed the leashed strength within him, and Lory was afraid. Afraid of what he might do. She put her hand to her throat, almost as if to protect it, and was silent.

Then Grant smiled. 'Well now,' he said. 'You've nothing to say for yourself? Strange, that. You are so full of confidence one moment, and now let me look at you. Well, well. You're just a wee girl after all. Nothing to worry about.' And he put his hand out and touched her cheek, and turned her to face him. 'That's better,' he said. 'That's *much* better.'

She knocked his hand away. 'Don't *touch* me,' she breathed. 'Just don't *touch* me!' She was trying not to tremble.

'How will you stop me?' he mocked. 'We're all alone— look around you, there is not a soul for miles. So how brave are you now, with all your fine talk and your patronizing manner? Tell me that—wee girl.'

She forced herself to look into his eyes, the dark deep blue of them, almost hypnotic in their depths, and she sensed the controlled anger within him. 'You don't frighten me,' she said slowly, summoning all her courage. 'Do you think that you do?'

'I don't know. You tell me. Why is your hand shaking so? Is it because I touched you? Is that what a man's touch can do to you?'

'Men don't frighten me,' she answered. 'Not *real* men.'

'Meaning I'm not?' He laughed. 'Now that's a dangerous thing to say to a Hebridean. I might be tempted to prove it.'

Lory turned away. She knew better than to speak. 'Is that what you meant?' he said again, as if he would have an answer from her whether she liked it or not. '*Dia*, you don't know what a real man is at all, for I doubt if you have met any down there in that city they call London. I have been there, and I've seen them with their long hair, and narrow shoulders——'

'There are other kinds!' she shot back.

'Och yes! Bowlers and pin-stripes and their umbrellas neatly rolled up in case a drop of rain should touch them. *Dia*! Is that your kind?' He began to laugh, a deep full-throated laugh—and it was the last straw for Lory. Her flying arm caught his shoulder, for he lifted it as if by instinct—and the impact jarred her, so hard was his body, and it was, in a way, like a repetition of something that had happened before in the Range-Rover, but Lory was too furious to know, or care—or even remember. And he never stopped laughing. Not even when he had taken hold of her arms, so that she was completely helpless, spitting fire and fury at him, squirming in impotent rage.

'Let me *go*!' she shouted.

'That's it,' he grinned at her, laughter spent. 'Now you are showing your true colours. Did you think you could hit me? Ach, but you've a fine temper on you, and you'll need to calm down before I let you go. Why, you're no stronger than a kitten, for all your fancy talk——'

'You beast!' She leaned her head forward, to try and bite him, and he jerked his hand—and her own—nearer himself. His eyes glinted.

'So I'm a beast now, am I? I might as well behave like one. This is what you expect, isn't it?' And before she could begin to even guess his intentions, he had pulled her strongly towards him—and then he kissed her.

He kissed her not once, or twice, but more, and he was not gentle—nor was he brutal, but each kiss was harder than the last, and he knew what he was about, that was for sure, and when he had finished with her, Lory collapsed, exhausted, her mouth afire with the hardness of his lips, her whole body trembling.

Then he released her, and put both his hands on her cheeks, and held her face so that she was forced to look at him. His eyes were dark and shadowed, narrowed, and he looked hard at her and said: 'Where's the fight gone now? Don't say you've never been kissed before?'

'You—I hate you! You're a *brute*!' Her voice was shaky.

'A beast—a brute—what next? I'm almost tempted to try——'

'You dare! You dare touch me again and I'll—I'll——'

'You'll what? Ach, you're all talk. You think I want to kiss you again? I have better things to do. Like doing some work. So stop your shaking and trembling and we'll go. Just be careful what you say to me in future, that's all. You'll maybe find I know a few more tricks than you when it comes to it. Remember that.' And he started the engine.

Lory, seething, her brain a mass of conflicting thoughts, sat beside him. She wanted to jump out of the Range-Rover, but he was going a shade too fast for that—she wanted to hurt and humiliate him in retaliation for what he had just done to her—but she dared not, for he wasn't playing games, he was deadly serious—and she knew who would be the loser in any further battle.

It was time to compose herself, before they reached their destination—wherever that might be. She felt as if she needed all her wits about her.

She began to breathe slowly and calmly in a deliberate effort to steady herself, and nearly succeeded. And when he stopped, and opened his door, she followed suit, jumping down on to rough ground. Then she looked around her. There was nothing to see, just the bleak hills, the track petering out in front of them—then nothing. No houses, no signs of life, not even a sheep. Alarm flared in her eyes, and he saw, and he laughed. 'Come away now, wee Lory. We have some walking to do.' And he strode away past the end of the track and along, and up, walking nimbly, not waiting for her. She had the awful sensation that if she remained there, the ground would swallow her up, and she would just simply vanish. Quickly, still confused and disturbed, she began to follow him.

Overhead gulls shrieked a mocking chorus, and she could hear the distant roar of the sea, and she had never felt so desolate, so completely *alone*, in all her life. And Grant, way ahead, began to whistle. Faintly familiar, Lory recognized it as the tune Mrs. Campbell had played on Saturday. Yet he wasn't taking her there. Where were they going? She concentrated on that question, instead of thinking about the startling events of their journey. For it was open war now, on both sides, and if she dared brood, she would be lost before she started. But what of Sister Monroe? What had he done? She could put nothing past him now— nothing. He was hard, and ruthless, and—stop! she told herself. I am *not* going to think about him. I am *not*. Grant stopped at the top of a rise, and looked down at her, and called:

'Nearly there now. You're not tired, I hope?'

'Go to hell!' she muttered, but under her breath. He waited until she had nearly reached him, and he was grinning.

'That's it. Walking is good exercise, you know. Tones up the muscles gently——'

'Spare me the lecture. I do know,' she answered shortly, saving her breath.

'I was just making conversation,' he said, all injured innocence.

'You wouldn't know how,' she snapped.

'Would I not? Ach, then you've never heard me in action. I can converse on most subjects I care to—even on sociology—does that surprise you?'

'I couldn't really care less,' she retorted. 'So why not save your talk for the people we're going to see?'

'They wouldn't be interested in such a profound subject.

123

They're simple folk—the kind you expected to meet on Creagdubh, in fact. Their main concerns are in growing their food, looking after their animals, and generally speaking, in surviving, in this harsh place. That's the kind of thing you hoped to see, is it not?' There was that something in his voice again; the air of mockery that raised her hackles. He was too near the truth for her comfort. Was he a mind-reader? Lory didn't answer. But her curiosity was thoroughly aroused. Where on earth could they be going?

A few minutes later they were there. The croft lay below them, and behind it was a hen-house, and a small walled garden, and in front of it was the sea. Similarly sited to the Campbells, in fact, looking out to the water as theirs did, but painted white, and with smoke issuing cheerfully from the chimney, and with several hens busily pecking at the stony ground.

'The Macdonalds live here,' said Grant. 'And they'll have a few dozen eggs for me, and maybe a chicken or two—and in return, I supply them with other essentials like oats and flour—free of charge. It's a system called barter—you'll maybe have heard of it, and it works very well. Don't forget to write *that* down in your little book,' and he strode off down the slope towards the front door of the croft. Seething, Lory followed.

The Macdonalds were in great contrast to the Campbells. Mrs. Macdonald opened the door for them, a cheerful plump body who greeted Lory with smiles of welcome, and assured her in her gentle lilting English that she was delighted to meet her. Inside the house was warmth and cheer, and a huge labrador sprawled by the fire.

'Callum is away looking to the sheep,' she said, beaming at Grant and Lory, 'but he'll no' be long, I don't doubt. Well now, how do you find Creagdubh, Miss Stevenson? Is it as you thought it would be?'

Grant, leaning against a huge sideboard, watched her with a bland expression on his face. 'It's a beautiful island, Mrs. Macdonald,' Lory assured her, certain in the knowledge that this woman would know exactly who she was, and why she was here.

'Aye, it is that. Well, sit you both down and I'll have the tea made in no time at all.'

'I'll get on with the work,' said Grant, 'and leave you to talk. You can shout me when the tea's ready,' and he went out into the kitchen, and closed the door behind him. The kettle bubbled on the fire, and the teapot stood in the hearth. Mrs. Macdonald picked up a huge square tin from the mantelpiece. It was a Coronation tea caddy with photos of King George VI and Queen Elizabeth, surrounded by Union Jacks. She spooned tea liberally into the pot, and the dog moved away warily as she lifted up the heavy kettle.

Sounds of hammering came from the kitchen, and the woman smiled at Lory. 'He doesn't waste time, that one,' she said. 'We were expecting him this morning, and it's a nice surprise that he has brought you as well. We see few visitors out here, and Grant is always welcome.'

'How do you get to the village?' Lory enquired.

'Ach, we walk!' She seemed surprised. 'It's not far at all—not over the hills. Ye'll have come the long way round by road, of course, but it takes us no time at all the way we go,' and she beamed warmly at Lory. 'Of course, sometimes he'll take us back with him, if we need to go to the Post Office, and then we'll visit all our friends in the village and have a good old natter.' Bright blue eyes regarded Lory thoughtfully. 'Everyone knows of your visit here, of course, for it doesna' take much time for news to travel hereabouts—there is so little of it,' and she chuckled richly. 'So as you can imagine, I was looking forward to meeting you. Aye well, they were right enough about one thing.' And she nodded and smiled.

'Oh! What was that?' Lory's seething rage against Grant was vanishing in the face of the warm welcome here, and Mrs. Macdonald's smile was one of pure friendliness—and something more, just faint, but there.

125

'Why, how pretty you are!'

'Oh! Thank you!' Lory was startled. Who could have said that? Not Grant, that was for sure.

Mrs. Macdonald laughed. 'And you're here to see how we live, aren't you?' she went on. 'Aye, well, you can see us here now, the life is a good one—not easy, mind, but we manage well enough.'

'I'm sure you do,' said Lory warmly. 'But is it never lonely for you, living so far away from neighbours?'

'Ach no! We have the wireless.' She said it as if that was sufficient in itself. '*And* we go visiting an odd evening or two. You'll not have been to a *ceilidh* yet, will you?'

'A—cayley?' The word sounded faintly familiar.

'Aye, that's the Gaelic for a party, a get-together, you might say. Och, we often have one in the village—but you'll not have been here long enough to go to one. Ah, then you'll see how we Gaels are,' and she shook her head. 'There's the music for a start—ach, it's good to hear the fiddles and the pipes going and everyone tapping their feet and singing——' she paused, listening intently. The sounds of hammering had ceased. 'Aye well, I'll pour out the tea.' And she opened the kitchen door and went out, leaving Lory to think. To think about whether Grant had stopped hammering to listen to their conversation—and to reflect that everyone on the entire island must know all about her. It was an odd feeling to have.

She could hear their voices in the kitchen, and then Mrs. Macdonald returned with a laden tray. 'He'll be in in a minute,' she told Lory. 'He's a good man, is Grant, I don't know what we'd do without him. He's putting up some shelves for us just now—if I waited for my husband to do them, I'd wait for ever, but he doesna' mind, and he's a good worker, as well as being a good landlord.'

She seemed oblivious of the fact that Grant could possibly hear her, and Lory nodded, and smiled—and wondered what he was thinking out there in the kitchen. If he had planned it that everyone should sing his praises he could hardly have done it better. But he hadn't, of course, it had just happened that way.

Then he was in the room again. He moved silently for such a big man, thought Lory. Silently, like a cat. And equally unpredictable.

'Well now,' he said, as he sat down balancing his cup and saucer precariously on his knee, as he took the proffered oatcake from Mrs. Macdonald, 'will you be making the games on Saturday?'

'Och, of course! We wouldn't miss them for anything!' she exclaimed, laughing. 'You'll be going too, Miss Stevenson?'

'Please call me Lory. Oh yes, Jean told me about them this morning. They sound very interesting.'

'Aye, they are that! You'll be entering for the bagpipes, Grant, then?'

The bagpipes! Lory's eyes widened, and she saw his mouth twitch, as if at her reaction, but he answered calmly enough: 'Och, I will that. But not the caber, not this year.'

'Ach well, no, you'll be giving that a rest,' agreed Mrs. Macdonald, nodding.

Lory could not resist it. 'Oh dear,' she said—very sweetly. 'Why not?' She should have known. She really should have known.

Grant looked modestly down at his plate. 'Well, it's only fair for someone else to have a chance,' he said, and Mrs. Macdonald finished it for him.

'Aye, you see, he's won it three years running—that's fair enough.' Lory looked up to see Grant's bland innocent gaze resting on her. His eyes said it all for him. They said: Let's see what clever answer you've got to *that*!

She smiled. 'How—interesting,' she said faintly.

'It is,' Mrs. Macdonald went on, clearly unaware of the subtle undercurrents in the room. 'I tell you now, you'd be good enough to beat anyone at *any* Highland Games, if you chose.' She looked at Lory. 'Why, it's a pity you'll not be seeing him in action this year. It's wonderful he is——'

Why, thought Lory, listening to Mrs. Macdonald's eulogy, he's sitting there laughing inside fit to burst. He's loving every minute of it, the conceited beast!

She was itching to change the subject, and managed it when their hostess went for more milk. Before she could start on again about Grant's skill in everything, it seemed, from caber tossing to shelf building, she said: 'Will the Campbells be going?'

There was a moment's silence while Mrs. Macdonald gave Grant a look. It was he who answered for her. 'They never go anywhere,' he said.

'And it's a right shame,' added Mrs. Macdonald. 'But there now, what can we do? She never speaks to anyone, the puir wee soul.'

Lory would never know what made her say what she did then. Perhaps reaction against the praise she'd been forced to listen to, about a man she didn't like—perhaps something else. Whatever it was, she simply said, very quietly: 'I wonder if she would if I asked her?' Even as the words came out, she felt the shock impact of them, but they were said then.

'You!' exclaimed Mrs. MacDonald. 'But you don't know what she's like——' and Grant interrupted, quite quietly, for him:

'I wonder?' He turned to the older woman, and something lit his eyes. 'It's maybe not as daft as it sounds, Mrs. Macdonald.' He turned then to Lory. 'I think—if anyone could—you could,' he said.

Lory sat very still, almost wishing she hadn't had the mad impulse. And yet—and yet not quite regretting it, for Mrs. Macdonald's face changed.

'How?' she asked him simply.

'We were there on Saturday,' he began, and Lory listened as he told of what had happened, and of the piano playing, and it brought it all back to her, but strangely enough as seen through another person's eyes, and a tiny

128

shiver ran down her spine at the hearing of it again, for she had sensed then a rapport with that little grey woman, a kind of sympathy when they had spoken of music—and it was clear that Grant was well aware of it too, for it came out in his words. When he had finished, Mrs. Macdonald was almost serious.

'And will you be going to them today?' she asked.

'I wasn't—but why?'

'Because I'd send some eggs. I think you are maybe right, Grant. The Lord knows, it would be a miracle—but they do happen, don't they?' and she smiled at Lory and patted her arm. 'You will do a lot of good for a sad woman if you can persuade her,' she said gently. 'More than you could imagine.'

'Then I'll try,' answered Lory. 'I'll do my best.' She even managed to smile at Grant. It was almost as if a truce existed in their battle.

'I should never have said anything,' she thought, as they scrambled down the steep bank to the Campbells'. She wasn't aware that she had spoken out loud until Grant answered her.

'Aye, but you did,' he answered, and waited for her to reach him. 'And I'm not sorry you did—you may be right after all. Who knows?'

He was carrying a bag full of eggs, very carefully, and he looked at Lory. 'I meant what I said back there at the Macdonalds',' he added. 'There was something when you went on Saturday. She took to you.'

'I bet that surprised you,' said Lory dryly, unable to help herself.

He laughed. Then he looked at her again, and said nothing, merely walked on. The look—and the laugh—had said more than words could. She glared at his broad back, and her mouth tightened. He was quite insufferable! But they were nearly there, and it was no use wasting time disliking him when, in a way, there was work to be done. She took a deep breath. Could she do it? Could she succeed where others had failed? She was going to have a good try.

And then, just before they reached the house, Grant did a surprising thing. He touched Lory's arm, quite gently, making her pause.

'Good luck,' he said quietly.

'Thanks.' For a moment, it was as if there were a bond between them. And it was strangely satisfying. They walked on, and he knocked at the door, and then they waited.

I shall soon be awash with tea, thought Lory, as they sat by the fire with Mrs. Campbell. Her husband had made it, and Lory took her cup from him with thanks, and refused a scone with the excuse that it was too near to lunch.

'It's just that we were at the Macdonalds',' explained Grant, 'and she insisted we bring you some eggs.'

Mrs. Campbell flushed. 'It's very kind of her,' she began, and gave her husband a look of desperate appeal.

'Aye, that it is. I'll away and thank them later,' he said.

'Can I have a word with you, John?' said Grant. 'About the roof?' An imperceptible signal must have passed between them, for John Campbell stood up immediately.

'Aye, come along, then. What was it you wanted to say?' Their voices faded as they went out through the kitchen and closed the back door after them. This was it. Lory and Mrs. Campbell were alone.

'I've been thinking about your piano since I played it on Saturday,' said Lory, smiling gently at the little woman. 'I did so enjoy playing. You didn't mind, did you?'

Mrs. Campbell went faintly pink. 'Why, no, of course not,' she said. 'It was nice to hear someone—to hear you play.' She looked across at it in the corner.

'It's nice,' she repeated, 'to hear someone else——' she stopped.

'Then can I have another go?' asked Lory. Whatever contact would be made between them, and it was at present a fragile thing, just as fine as a spider's web, would be through music, she sensed that instinctively.

'Aye, if you like. Of course.'

'You have some music?'

'There's some in the stool. Lift the lid.'

Lory did so, and found some very old sheet music from years past, yellowed with age, some of it, and she looked through, fascinated, and found Mrs. Campbell beside her. Together they went over the music, and Lory prayed that the men would not return, for the other woman was coming to life, she could feel it, could almost know what she would say next.

'Would you—would you like to try this one?' It was a tune from the thirties, and Lory had never heard of it, but she took the paper and opened it, and looked down at the notes.

'I'll try,' she said, smiling. 'I'll certainly try.' She looked at Mrs. Campbell. 'Is it a favourite of yours?'

'Aye—it was. But I'd forgotten about it.'

It was a catchy tune, entitled 'Flapperette,' and Lory flexed her fingers and, tentatively at first, began to play.

There was a moment's silence when she had finished, and then Mrs. Campbell shook her head. 'Fine,' she whispered. 'Just fine. Och, I mind well when I first played it.' And she was almost smiling. Not quite, but near enough.

'Play something for me,' Lory begged. 'Anything you like.'

'Och no——'

'Please. You have a wonderful touch.' And she went and sat on a little footstool by the piano, and waited, holding her breath.

'Well——' Mrs. Campbell sat herself down and stroked the keys gently. Then softly, hesitantly, she began to play, and the magic notes filled the room, and Lory listened intently, then relaxed, because she knew, she just *knew*, that everything was going to be all right. She didn't know how she was going to do it, but she was going to persuade Mrs. Campbell to go to the games. Somehow she would find the words. She *had* to.

CHAPTER NINE

'You must be a witch,' remarked Jean, passing Lory a cup of tea. 'How did you do it? And what did Grant have to say about *that*?' It was Thursday, and Lory was beginning to wonder if she could take another two weeks on Creagdubh. Never had she thought that there could be so much to do, so many places to go, on such a small island.

She rubbed her aching shoulder, souvenir of a fishing trip with Finlay and Grant the previous day. 'I don't know how I did it,' she confessed, 'except that I was determined to do so. It seemed so important to everybody, I'd not have been able to face myself—or Grant—if I failed. So when we'd been talking music for a little while I told her about being asked to go to the games, and I implied—it was a white lie in a good cause—that I was dying to go, but was simply too shy, not knowing anyone properly—but that I'd go quite happily as long as I knew she was going. I pretended, you see, that I'd assumed she was going—and when she looked as though she was going to faint and told me that she never went, I just said something like "what fun. It'll be the first time for both of us"—or something like that. I honestly can't remember the exact words, Jean,' she took a swallow of hot tea, 'because in a way it was like being in a sort of dream, kind of unreal, but I remember taking her hand and saying please wouldn't she go for me, and the next moment she took a deep breath, looked as if she might burst into tears, and then said—yes.'

Lory stopped, moved at the memory of it all, even in the telling of it. 'And as for Grant, you'll have to ask him what *he* thinks, because we're not exactly speaking to each other, because he can't *stand* me, and what puzzles me is why he takes me places—except, of course, to keep an eye on me and know exactly what I'm up to.'

'Hmm!' said Jean, and her mouth twitched. 'So that's how it is!'

'That's precisely how it is, and he's also trying to exhaust me in the process—and succeeding, I might add. It's jolly nice just to be sitting here, I can tell you.'

'And it's lovely to have you, believe me. I'll be sorry when you leave, Lory. I'll really miss you.' Then she added, very casually, almost as an afterthought:

'And can't you stand him either?'

The back of Lory's neck prickled. 'He doesn't exactly bring me out in a rash, but near enough. I can feel my hackles rise just thinking about him.'

'Is that a fact? Tsk! What a shame, Lory. He can be so nice, you know.'

'Yes—but not to me. He makes that clear. Still, I shouldn't grumble. I'm seeing everywhere—and everyone, or near enough. I'm not really getting anywhere because everyone seems to talk about *him* all the time, but,' she shrugged, '—it's passing the time, I suppose. Don't get me wrong,' she added hastily. 'I love coming here to visit *you*—and Finlay and the others, but I've never had such a frustrating job, work-wise, in my life.'

Jean laughed. 'Then treat it as a holiday! Think of work when you get back to London. Ach, you canna' do that here at all. The air is too fresh, the atmosphere too timeless, in a way. We don't hurry here to timetables and such, life is at a steady pace, you'll find—if you were here long enough.'

'But he works hard, Grant, I mean,' Lory put in. 'He never seems to stop, in a way. Even though I don't like him, I've got to admit that.'

'Aye, you have to admit that,' answered Jean, giving Lory such an odd look that she was prompted to ask:

'What—what are you getting at, Jean?'

'Och, nothing!' Jean's face was a picture of innocence.

'Nothing at all—only——' she stopped.

'Only?' prompted Lory.

'Only are you really *sure* you can't stand each other? *Really* sure?'

The question wasn't what Lory had expected, and for a moment she was silent. Then she answered, quickly—too quickly: 'I would have thought it was obvious!'

'Aye, that's just it,' remarked Jean blandly. 'It is obvious—on his part, anyway. You're maybe more subtle. But Grant—well now. I just don't know what to make of him at all, and that's a fact.'

'I'm not sure what you mean.' Lory traced a pattern with her finger on the tablecloth. She didn't look at Jean.

'Nor am I really,' Jean admitted. 'Except that I've never seen him *bristle* like he does with you, not with anyone else, that is. Why, he has good manners, has our laird, it is inborn in someone like that, as natural to them as breathing, and yet, well—it's most strange, and that's all I can say about it, and *that*'s a fact!'

'I vote we don't waste any more time talking about him anyway,' said Lory with a firmness she did not feel. 'Tell me about the games, and how we'll all get there, to start with.'

'Och, we go by boat, of course,' said Jean. 'It's a big one—Iain's fishing boat. And we'll set off early, about eight, so as to have a good long day, and we take sandwiches because I've got a lot of mouths to feed, and it's easier that way than queuing up by the tent—you'll have some with us, will you?'

'Of course. Thank you—but only if you'll let me help you get everything ready. Shall I come down Friday night?'

'That would be nice. Then you'll meet Iain at last. I'm sorry you've kept missing him, but he goes far afield fishing, and it's a good time of year for that. We live according to the seasons here. I make all my preserves at this time of year, and salt the herrings for winter when there's no chance of going out——' Lory listened fascinated to this slice of island life, the simplicity of the way in which Jean painted the picture of their way of living. Harsh it might appear to anyone such as herself, but it had its own values and advantages.

She left Jean eventually to go to the Post Office for stamps and cards, and to walk back to Creagdubh House for lunch, for Grant had not appeared, and Jean would have the children arriving any time for their meal. It was better to be independent of him if she could, she reflected, as she walked briskly along after her brief stop at the village's only shop. There had been a slight thaw in the post-mistress's attitude—a prickly little busybody who was clearly a friend of Elspeth's, and therefore no friend of Lory's. She had wondered why, briefly, and then discovered as she was leaving why it should be so. As Miss Carmichael had handed her her change, she had said:

'It is a good thing you have done for Mrs. Campbell,' and she had smiled, actually smiled, as she said it. It left Lory with a warm glow, a sense of achievement. There was no longer any surprise in her that all her actions were general knowledge. There was a spring in her step as she walked along the track to Creagdubh House. At least, she thought, my visit to this island won't be entirely useless! For in every other respect, regarding her job, she might as well not have bothered. She wondered when she would hear from her father. No doubt he would be expecting her to be half way through her book by now. Lory smiled wryly to herself. He hadn't met Grant, though.

She heard the Range-Rover long before it came into view, and paused at the roadside as he drove up from behind her. The passenger door was flung open, and he shouted: 'Get in!' Then he looked at her.

'I thought you were waiting for me at Jean's,' he said.

'I was,' she answered sweetly, 'but when it got to twelve I decided you'd forgotten me, so I set off walking.'

He changed gear and they set off. 'Hmm, I'd have a job

to do *that*, wouldn't I?' he answered. 'I was delayed, that's all.'

She was definitely not going to argue with him. 'I've arranged to go to Jean's on Friday night and help her get ready for the boat trip to the games,' she told him. 'Because she tells me it's an early start on Saturday.'

'Aye, it is. Well, I'll run you, then——'

'I wasn't asking for a lift, I was just telling you,' she remarked.

'I know fine, you weren't. But I'll take you anyway. And on Saturday I'll be going for the Campbells about seven. You'll come with me?'

'Yes, of course. You don't think—she'll change her mind?'

'I don't know. That's why it's better you come too.'

Lory was silent for a minute as they bumped along the hard ground. In a way, she had a big responsibility. She had started something, quite unwittingly, something that had apparently become as big a talking point on the island as her own presence there. Mrs. Campbell never left her home, had not done so for years. She, Lory, had persuaded her to do so. It was as simple as that. But it wasn't really simple at all. For if Mrs. Campbell did go to the games—*if* she didn't change her mind at the last minute, which was a strong possibility—then, Lory knew, she would have achieved something not far short of a miracle. And that was a sobering thought in itself. She looked down at her hands. She hoped it would happen. For then, whatever else happened on this island, she would go away in two weeks with a sense of achievement. Two weeks. That was all that remained. Just fourteen more days, and then farewell, Creagdubh, and all the people on it. Just for a second, Lory felt as if she had been here all her life. The feeling passed in an instant, but it left an awareness behind it, inside her. And she remembered it later, in her room that evening.

Lory stood by the window late that evening, just looking

out at the rocks being pounded by the restless sea, and remembered what had happened earlier in the day.

Supper was over. A few hardy souls had gone for a walk in the soft rain which pattered on her window, for it was their last evening, and tomorrow they would be taking the plane home. Not Edna and Joan. They had another week, as had Ellis and Raymond, but others, that she scarcely knew except to pass the time of day at meals. Lory suddenly felt very restless. She had walked back to the village after lunch to post her cards to friends, and had visited Finlay. He had been pleased, she knew that as soon as she had gone in, and her visit had been a pleasant, satisfying one. She had told him far more about herself than she had anyone else, because in his company she felt truly at home, and relaxed. They had sat by his fire drinking tea and eating home-made biscuits, and the time had passed quickly. He had told her of his life when a younger man, his travels round the world on merchant ships, before the accident which had robbed him of his sight. 'And then,' he said, 'I came home to Creagdubh, as we all do eventually. I came home to die, because I thought that without my sight there was nothing left to live for—but then I found out that I had more friends here than I had ever had in all my journeys around the world, and I began to live again. Home is where the heart is, Lory, and that may be a trite old saying, but *Dia*, it is so very true. I have a richness and contentment here that I never found on my travels. Ach, you should be here for the *ceilidhs*, and you would know. There I can play my fiddle, and I hear the others dancing and I know that I could never leave this place again ...'

He had gone on at length, and she had listened, deeply moved by his quiet sincerity, and glad that a lump in the throat was not visible—but perhaps he knew, with his keen perception, for he had held her hand when it was time for her to go, and had said: 'You will come again? I sense that I have found another friend in you, my dear.' And she had promised, and gone then.

138

His words came back to her now. Home is where the heart is. His heart was in Creagdubh, and he would never leave it. So was Grant's. He too had seen the world, and knew what it was like, but when the time had come, he had returned here and taken over from his great-uncle. So what was the magic which held them fast? Lory closed her eyes, for it was as if she knew. She had known it in that brief instant when she felt as if she had been here all her life. She shivered, and turned away from the window. It was no use, she knew she wouldn't sleep. She was too restless.

She unrolled her mackintosh from its corner of the wardrobe, shook it out, and put on her coat. A good walk in the rain should do it—she hoped.

She took a detour after walking down to the gate and along the rough road for a way. She began to climb the hill to the sea, with the intention of reaching Creagdubh House again from the kitchen garden side. It was not dark enough to have to keep to the known tracks, for even in the rain, visibility was good. There was something quite exhilarating in feeling the cold drops on her face and she raised it to the sky and licked them from her lips. It even tasted different from London rain, almost sweet. She smiled at her imagination, for rain was rain the world over—but still—the thought remained, and she remembered something her grandmother had told her when she was a child. That hair washed in rainwater was always softer and cleaner. Her grandmother had lived in a cottage in Berkshire, and there had been a rain barrel by the back door, and from this she had taken panfuls of water when hair-washing time came round. And her grandmother's white hair had always been beautifully silky. On an impulse, Lory whipped off her plastic headscarf and shook her hair free. 'Come on, rain!' she called, 'soak my hair, and let's see how true it is!' It was as if a kind of madness had come over her. The fact that there was nowhere to dry her hair bothered her not at all. She just didn't *care* any more.

She went on through scrubby heather and grass, and she

was almost running now, filled with a strange kind of reck-lessness. She was truly alone, not a soul in sight, and even the sheep were sensible enough to be huddling somewhere for shelter. And then—she was too near the cliff edge, and she halted, suddenly sober. If she had run on, just kept going as she had been doing, she would have been over the top, and dashed on to the rocks below. She looked down and went almost dizzy. The roar of the sea filled her ears, filled her mind and senses so that she was almost at one with it. The sea, hypnotizing, inexorable—she moved away, and back, and now she was trembling with reaction. How foolish she had been!

Quieter, she began walking to the left, to where the lights of Creagdubh House glimmered faintly in the distance, a welcoming haven in the dusk, blurred with the rain that filled her eyes, but there, solid and immovable as the rocks themselves. There for ever. Scrambling, less surefooted—or foolhardy—now, Lory made her way back.

Then she heard something, and a tingle of disbelief touched her spine. She heard the faint sound of bagpipes coming from the direction of the house. It was haunting, evocative, and very sad, and she stood still, the better to hear it, for she was a distance away, and although sound carried clearly, the rain lent a blurred softness to the notes, so that they had an almost magical quality to them, almost as though it was the music of the island, with no human agency responsible. She shook off the absurd fancy in-stantly, for there were no ghosts here.

It would be Grant, of course. Who else? And he would be rehearsing for the games the day after next, which was natural enough, and there was nothing ghostly about *him*, that was for sure. Slowly, Lory began walking towards the house, and the sounds came more clearly now; the tune changed, and he was playing 'Amazing Grace,' and some-how it was more beautiful than she had ever heard it before, and she suddenly wanted to cry.

The wall of the vegetable garden was ahead of her, and

behind it she could see the outbuildings, and then the house itself, and the rain was coming more heavily so that her head and face were drenched, but it all seemed to fit in with her mood, which was suddenly, inexpressibly sad. Lory paused, for here she could not possibly be seen by anyone in the house, and she wanted to listen to the music before she at last went in. Music? She had never liked bagpipes. People made jokes about them, talked about the wailing of them—but it was music, and it was not funny, it was truly beautiful, and fitting in perfectly with the bleak, harsh surroundings, bathing them in a glow of colour she had not thought to see.

The tune had changed to 'Scotland the Brave,' and it was the time for Lory to go in and get to her room before he found her listening. And it was time for her to try and do something with her drenched hair. If she went the long way round to the front it would take at least ten minutes over rocky ground. But to slip through the gate, quickly cross the gardens and then curve round against the wall of the house would take one, or two, at the most. And he was fully engrossed now in belting out 'Scotland the Brave.' He wouldn't see her. Lory opened the gate, closed it behind her, and walked quickly along the narrow path between rows and rows of growing vegetables—potatoes, cabbage, lettuce, sprouts, cucumbers—some under frames, some protected by plastic sheeting, all looking remarkably healthy and verdant. Against the wall of Creagdubh House itself was a greenhouse, and inside, tall tomato plants reached proudly to the roof. She suddenly realized that the delicious tomato soup she so enjoyed was home-made. And why not? There were enough growing there to feed not only the entire island, but probably a small army as well. Who tended them? Grant, of course. Grant Mackinnon, Laird of Creagdubh, protector of birds, fisherman, caber tosser, bagpipe player, green-fingered gardener, landlord, roof repairer —and probably dozens of other things besides that Lory couldn't begin to imagine. Quietly, walking quickly, huddling now against the lashing, ceaseless rain, she went towards the house; in her mind a jumble of multi-coloured pictures, images of Grant. Grant the Provider——

'Lory!' His voice, harsh and deep, cut into her mind, and she stopped, feeling muddled and suddenly insecure as the kilted figure came towards her from the outbuilding.

'What on earth are you doing?' he demanded.

Lory lifted her chin. She didn't like his tone. Did he think she was trespassing? Pinching a few cabbages for private consumption? 'Taking a short cut to the house,' she answered. 'Why?'

'You're drenched, woman,' he said. '*Dia*, but you look like a kitten dragged from the sea!'

'Thanks,' she muttered. 'And if you keep me talking much longer I'll be even wetter, won't I?' and she clenched her teeth to stop herself from hurling further insults at him, and turned to walk away—but he took hold of her arm.

'This way,' he said. 'That gate to the front of the house is stiff. Come away through the kitchen with me.'

'No, *thanks*!' She tried to pull her arm free, but it had as much effect as a branch trying to wrench itself from its tree.

'Ach, come on. I've no time to stand chatting here with you. I'm getting wet too, you know.' And he turned and marched her towards the back door. Lory panicked. Elspeth would be there. Elspeth! who was bad enough at mealtimes but would be doubly so at seeing a bedraggled Lory frog-marched through her precious kitchen dripping rain all over her clean floor. And then, as they neared the massive archway inside which was the door, a kind of fatalistic calm came over Lory. What did it matter? Elspeth's opinion could hardly drop any lower than it already had. She, Lory, would just give her a pleasant smile and wish her good evening, and see how *that* took her.

They were inside the porch now, and it was dark, and cool, but mercifully dry.

'Take off your mac,' Grant commanded. 'I'll hang it here

to drip. You can have it back in the morning.'

'Yes, sir.' She obeyed promptly. 'Where are your bag-pipes?'

'I've left them in the shed. No use in ruining them.'

'No, of course not.' She handed him her mackintosh. 'There you are—sir.'

'Are you being sarcastic?' he enquired, gently for him.

She looked shocked. 'Who, me? Heavens, no. It's just that you're giving so many orders it seemed the right way to address you.'

He looked down at her. Reached his arm out and hung the dripping plastic on to a nearby peg, then he smiled. A slow smile that was reflected in his dark eyes as he stood watching her. 'Aye, well,' he said. 'It's strange to hear someone such as yourself accepting orders—but there you are—no doubt Creagdubh has tamed you somewhat, and that can be no bad thing. Come away in now,' and he took her arm, pushed open the inner door, and they were in the kitchen before she had time to reply to his maddening insolence. Deftly, swiftly, in just a few words he had turned the tables on Lory. Instead of being disconcerted by her sarcasm he had shot it back at her in such a way that she now felt as if she had to explain herself. And of course, that was the last thing she could do. Not to him. Not ever. He was absolutely insufferable!

'It's only me, Elspeth,' he called, as the white-haired figure bustled out of the large pantry. 'I've brought Miss Stevenson in. She had lost her way at the back. Do you have that hair dryer that I mended for you a wee while ago?'

'But I——' began Lory.

'Aye. Somewhere. But I'm busy just now.' And Elspeth sniffed.

Grant was steering Lory towards the door to the hall. Succulent cooking smells tantalized her nostrils and made her hungry. 'Never mind. Off you go, Lory. You'll find your way from here, will you?' he enquired solicitously.

'Yes, thank you.' She did not wish to call him sir again. Somehow that little ploy had fallen on stony ground. She heard the door close behind her, and heard him begin to laugh, and she clenched her fists and ran up the stairs. She hoped she wouldn't meet anyone, because she didn't want to talk.

She kicked off her shoes, undressed, and put on her nightie and dressing gown, then began to rub her hair vigorously. The mad impulse had faded, to be replaced by a mood of almost depression. Her hair was absolutely wringing wet. Why on earth had she remembered that bit of folklore from her grandmother? She would probably catch pneumonia as a result, and die, and go to heaven with the words, 'But rainwater is good for the hair,' ringing in her ears like an angels' chorus. At that absurd thought Lory began to laugh. Might as well be hanged for a sheep as for a lamb, she thought, and fumbled in her dressing table drawer for a shampoo sachet. Friday night was generally hair washing night, but she'd be at Jean's tomorrow, so it might as well be done now, and if she had to sit up for hours while it dried naturally, better now than tomorrow, before an early start to the games. And she could always finish her notes.

The thought became the deed, and Lory went and filled the washbasin with hot water, tore the edge of the sachet off with her teeth, and began to wash her hair.

She was giving it a final rinse when the knock came at the door, and she froze, stood still where she was, and prayed that they—whoever they were—would go away. Gently, very carefully, not making a sound, she wrapped the towel turban-wise round her head, and turned away from the bowl to face the door. Go away! she willed silently. Go away, whoever you are, I do not want to talk.

'Lory? Are you there?' It was, of course, Grant. Who else would be so rude, so insensitive as to knock at her door at nearly midnight? Why, no one. Only *him*.

'No, I'm not here. Go away,' she whispered fiercely, and

heard him laugh. His ears were keen, that was obvious.

'I've brought you a present,' he said.

'Really? A bomb? Hand grenade? I'm trying to give them up. Please go away.'

'A hair dryer. Do you want it or don't you?'

'Oh!' She crossed to the door and opened it. 'Thank you. If you'll just put it on the bed, I'll manage——'

'No, you won't. That's what I want to explain, and why I didn't get Elspeth to bring it up——'

'Would she have come?' Lory interrupted dryly.

He ignored it. 'It's a bit tricky still. It's quite old, and you have to keep your finger on——'

'Does it work or not?' she cried out, exasperated.

He raised a cynical eyebrow. 'Och, dear now, there's a sharp tongue you have tonight! First you call me sir when it's quite obvious you would rather be calling me some other names, then you do not answer your door, and now you are beginning to sound very snappish. Not at all the behaviour we would expect from a lady sociologist——'

'We? Is that the royal "we"? You sound like Queen Victoria——'

'We—the islanders, that is, and indeed you are *very* sharp-tongued tonight. Is your wet hair depressing you? Better to get it dry——'

'Oh, go to——' But the last word was fortunately lost as Lory, most humiliatingly, began to sneeze. Not only that, but she couldn't stop, and had to sit down on the bed. Helplessly, her body racked with the spasms, she sat there, and saw Grant bend to a plug by her bed and fix the dryer to it. Then the room was filled—as well as with her sneezes—with the hum of the dryer, and she knew what he meant. It was old-fashioned all right. It was, in fact, positively ancient. It was like having a dynamo in the room with her. A mechanical, and a human dynamo, for what else was he?

'Turn round,' he commanded, and the next moment she felt a warm blast of air on her hair.

Sniffing, sneezing temporarily suspended, she gasped in

muffled tones:

'I can—ah—ah—can manage, thank you!'

'No, you—ah—ah—cannot,' he mimicked her efforts not to sneeze with a cruel relish. 'Because apart from the fact that you'd probably drop it in the middle of a hefty sneeze, you don't know where to keep your finger on, and you'd probably end up electrocuting yourself *and* setting the place on fire to boot, and that would be inconvenient because we don't have a fire brigade.'

'Inconvenient? Thanks,' she answered dryly. 'I'm touched by your concern for my safety.' But it was rather odd that he should be there holding the dryer to her hair. It was all so personal, and Lory began to find herself feeling distinctly uneasy. 'Er—may I get my brush?' she asked. The sneezes had subsided somewhat, leaving her patches of coherent speech, and if he wasn't going to go away, as seemed the case, then she might as well take full advantage of his actions, and get her hair dried properly.

'Of course.' He switched off, and the loud hum ceased, and in the silence that then filled the room they both heard the sounds of revelry from downstairs. Laughter, and the chink of glasses as those who were leaving the following day were consoled by those who were staying. And Lory suddenly realized something she had been subtly aware of all week, without being able to put it into words. Everyone who visited Creagdubh House loved it there—and came back again, sometimes year after year. It was not as if it were a busy seaside resort. There was no entertainment, not even television in the evenings, yet no one was ever bored or at a loss. The whole atmosphere of the island was so exhilarating, so challenging, that everyone who stayed there must feel it as she herself had done.

And she suddenly realized something else. She was standing at her dressing table lost in contemplation of these facts, and Grant was coughing discreetly. 'Eh—you canna' find your brush?' he asked politely, only not politely, as Lory knew, because she recognized every nuance in his voice, and

146

politeness was one of those little things that was noticeably absent in any remark he made to her.

'Yes. It's—ah—ah—here.' She successfully stifled another sneeze and walked back to the bed. 'Really, if you'll just *show* me. I'm sure I'll manage.'

'Not a chance. It'll no' take long.' Was it her imagination, or had his Hebridean accent become more pronounced, as if he knew it made her uneasy? For there was something so fascinating about the way everyone spoke there that Lory loved to hear it. Yet with him, subtly, it was different. For his voice was deep, and when he spoke, in the soft gentle lilt of the Hebrides, there was only one way to describe his tones. Sexy. She would have died rather than admit it, because of course she detested him, but she wondered, really wondered for a moment, if her toes were curling up. She choked back another sneeze at the idea.

She began to brush her hair, briskly dismissing such treacherous fancies. Then Grant's fingers touched hers briefly, and he said: 'Give the brush to me for a moment.'

'B—but—why——'

'Give it to me.'

Wordlessly, Lory obeyed. There didn't seem much point in arguing with him. She pulled her dressing gown more securely round her and waited. The next second he started the dryer again and began brushing her hair. Tugging gently, so that she had to tilt her head slightly back, and then, instead of standing, she felt his weight on the bed behind her, and her whole spine tingled in sheer astonishment. It didn't matter, it really didn't, that she disliked him and he disliked her, just at the moment she thought she had never experienced anything quite as delicious as what was happening to her now.

'Mmm,' she murmured, but he wouldn't hear it above the noise of the dryer. The brush travelled down her hair, and fanned it out slightly, and the warmth touched her scalp, and she tingled all over and was thankful that he could not see her face, for without a doubt it would give her away.

Minutes passed. Once he asked if it was all right, and she managed to answer somehow, and then, just as she was completely relaxed, he switched the dryer off, said: 'I must let it cool for a moment.'

Silence filled the room, except again for the renewed sounds of merriment downstairs. A ragged chorus of 'Auld Lang Syne' began and Lory saw rather than heard his wince, then quite gently, with no hint of what was to come in his voice, he said: 'Why do you go walking so foolishly in the rain when you are not used to it?' He was regarding the antiquated dryer as he spoke, touching it thoughtfully as if that was of the utmost importance, not his words.

Lory's nerve ends were raw. Sore with the restlessness that had made her go out in the first place, stung with Elspeth's negative reaction to his request for the hair dryer —and now fully tingling with the treacherous warmth of Grant's gentle touch on her hair, a touch that had set all her senses aflare with the knowledge that she was not completely invulnerable to him after all.

'Foolishly?' she snapped. 'It's the only thing to do, isn't it, seeing that no one will really tell me anything round here. At least I can talk to myself when I'm out, and not get silly answers.'

'Is that a fact?' he said mockingly. Anger rose swiftly in her at his patronizing tone. She had promised not to reveal Jean's secret, but there was another way.

'Oh, it's all right,' she answered, taking the brush up from the bed. 'I can *guess* why no one really talks to me—oh, it's all very civil and polite, but the conversation always turns to the state of the fishing—or how marvellous *you* are!'

And then he began to laugh softly, satisfied, and Lory, incensed, lashed out with: 'If you didn't read everybody's letters you might be more wonderful.'

There was an instant silence, and she could have bitten her tongue.

'*I* read your letters?' he said softly, and it was all the

148

more menacing for that. 'What made you think so?'

'Because I'd left a letter to my father telling him of my plans—and—and it was moved slightly when I came back from breakfast,' she lied desperately, to be sure that Jean would not be connected with her accusation.

'Aye, so you did. You wrote and told him you were planning a book about my island, and how interesting it would be to get everyone's feelings about living here "in depth," as I think you referred to it. As if, to you, we were just a load of specimens to be put in jars and labelled, and, *Dia*, I won't have any of that, so I went and told everyone what you were planning to do. I left it to them whether they told you about their lives or not—but I also made it clear that the whole idea displeased me. Aye, you're right there—but you're wrong about one thing. I have never read anyone else's letters in my life. It was not *me* who read it.'

CHAPTER TEN

'THEN it was——' Lory paused. She knew, of course, but she waited to hear it.

'Aye, it was Elspeth,' said Grant. 'Who else? Do you think she cares? She is loyal to me. If people go around leaving private matters on view for all to see they must expect them to be seen. I do not blame her—and you are not to say anything to her either, because you asked for it.'

Lory took a deep breath. 'It's all right,' she said. 'I've dropped the plan now. I shall do my job, what I came here to do, and that's all. So you should feel pleased with yourself.'

'Pleased?' He rolled the word round his tongue, amused. 'You can put it that way if you like. I don't really care one way or another any more. I consider you quite unimportant in my scheme of things. I told you once before—Creagdubh was here before you came and it will go on unchanged after you have gone. It is greater than both of us.'

He had stood up slowly as he spoke, and looked down at Lory, and the tension was now throbbing in the room. Quite suddenly it had happened, even as he had been speaking. The intensity of his words was a tangible force threatening her, frightening her. She moved, tried to stand, but he was too close.

Then, just as the silence had stretched on a taut thread to breaking point, the lights went out. And from downstairs came a startled roar, followed almost instantly by laughter —and Grant said: 'Stay there. It looks like a fuse.'

He opened the door, and his black shadowy shape went

out. Lory had no intention of moving. She was utterly shaken, in more than one way. The door was open. She could hear the jumbled laughter and remarks from below as everyone enjoyed the unexpected crisis, something to tell their friends about when they got home. Grant's footsteps had faded. A patch of grey light came from the window and she turned her head to watch it and listen to the rain making soft pattering noises against the glass. She sat there in the dark and wondered why there should be this tension, this awareness, whenever the two of them were alone together. Then the image of his face came in the darkness before her, in her mind's eye. And she thought she knew, and dismissed the idea as too absurd for words.

The lights came on again, making her blink, and she heard him bounding up the stairs, and she composed her features.

'All right? It was the fuses. Is your hair nearly dry? I must look at this dryer again, in case it was delayed reaction from that,' he said, and it was so terribly civilized, in complete contrast to the scene before that she wanted to cry out, to tell him to get out. But she didn't.

'Yes, thank you,' she said. He was aware of it too, she was sure of that.

'Fine. I'm going now. Good night.'

'Good night.'

He was gone, and Lory lay down on the bed, going over everything in her mind. Elspeth, not Grant, had read her letter. And tomorrow she would go to Jean's, and on Saturday they would all go to the games—and after that—after that—she could not stay on Creagdubh for another two weeks. It was impossible, and would be intolerable. She knew enough to make out a full report now. Enough basic *facts*. No more. But they would be enough.

On Monday—or Tuesday—whichever day the plane came, she intended to leave Creagdubh. For if she did not, she was very much afraid it would be too late.

*

Lory had never laughed so much in her life before. It was Friday evening, and she and Jean and Jean's husband Iain were in the living room of their house by the village. Grant had dropped her there shortly after dinner, and said he would return later. And now Lory had met Iain for the first time and knew why Sister Monroe had made a dead set for him, and knew why Jean always looked so cheerful—and knew too why he and Grant were friends.

Iain was big, of similar build to Grant, with a fresh ruddy-cheeked complexion and a hearty laugh—and an incredible sense of humour. The children were all in bed and there were just the three of them in the warm living room. And the jokes came from Iain at a speed that made her hold her sides and beg him to desist. Jean went on calmly slicing bread, for she had clearly heard them all before. Even so, her mouth twitched, and she occasionally had to whisper a warning hush at her husband as the laughter rose.

'Oh, please,' Lory pleaded. 'Please stop for a minute and let me get on with these sandwiches. That *is* what I came for tonight, you know.'

'Ach, you have just to stop listening to him, for he is like this all the time,' said Jean, with an affectionate sidelong glance at her spouse, who held a glass of whisky in his hand as he sat back comfortably in his fireside chair.

He raised his glass to her. 'Och, lassie, lassie, ye're making me blush with all these fine compliments,' he said, unabashed, and looking as though he had no intention of blushing.

'Aye well,' retorted Jean, 'you would be more use if you gave us a hand instead of sitting there with your wee dram.'

'I'm gathering my strength up for tomorrow,' he answered. 'Would you like me to fail in everything because I was too busy making sandwiches to have the rest I needed?' He looked at Lory and winked. 'My wife doesn't understand me at all.'

'Just leave me out of this,' begged Lory, busily spreading cream cheese on slices of crusty bread. 'I'm not taking sides. Just as long as I can get on with what I came to do——'

'There's a wise girl,' Iain told Jean. 'She'll make someone a good wifie, never arguing——' He was silenced by their burst of laughter.

'What have I said?' he demanded.

Jean and Lory exchanged a glance of complete understanding, made more so by Iain's look of total bewilderment. 'Never you mind,' said Jean, nodding. 'Just never you mind.'

'I think,' said Lory gently, 'that Jean means that although I may not argue with you——' and she paused.

'Aye? Go on,' he urged, putting his drink down.

'Well, I do with—with——' she stopped.

He nodded, as if sudden comprehension had dawned. 'Och, wait a minute—don't tell me, let me guess. Grant? Is that it?'

'It's none of your business,' said Jean firmly, slapping down a slice of bread.

'Och, it is that! So that's the way of it, is it?' He shook his head. 'Well, well. I thought the sparks were flying a bit when he brought you here. Now why should a peaceful man like Grant want to fight with a bonny lass like you?' He regarded her severely, only the glimmer of laughter in his eyes betraying him.

'It's a wonder he's not told you already,' said Lory. 'I should think he's told everyone else. He doesn't like sociologists—he doesn't like one sociologist in particular, namely—me.'

'It's only because you've a mind of your own,' said Jean soothingly. 'He's like all the men round here'—and she pulled a face at her husband—'old-fashioned enough to believe a woman's place is tied to the kitchen sink——'

'A terrible lie!' Iain exclaimed. 'Just because we are superior beings to you poor females——'

'See what I mean?' Jean demanded loudly. 'I'll hit him with the frying pan in a minute——'

'Just because,' Iain interrupted, 'of that fact of life, there's no need to go around slandering us. *We* can't help being cleverer than——' his words were lost, as Jean took a swipe at him with the tea towel from the table, and they all dissolved into laughter as he vainly tried to defend himself.

He stood up. 'Now, just to show there's no ill feeling,' he said, 'I'll make us all a cup of tea.' And he marched in a very dignified manner to the sink with the kettle, while Jean and Lory, still shaking, tried to finish the sandwiches.

Jean put her hand to her stomach. 'Oh dear,' she said, 'I really shouldn't let myself laugh so much.'

'You're all right?' asked Lory, alarmed.

'Och yes. Take no notice of me. Anyway, the baby's not due for three weeks.'

'Aye well, sit down anyway,' said Iain. 'I'll finish these off now. You watch the kettle.' And he made her sit in his chair and put the tea towel round his waist with a flourish. The sandwiches were finished at speed. He had a deft way with a knife, even if the slices were not quite as thin as Jean's, and the pile of bread mounted precariously as Lory struggled to keep up with him.

She privately thought they were making far too many sandwiches—a thought that was to return to her the following day when she saw them all vanishing at a fantastic rate.

Everything was done at last, sandwiches wrapped in foil, hardboiled eggs in a basket with tomatoes, all waiting neatly on the sideboard, and they sat down for that well-earned cup of tea, brewed and poured by Iain, who in spite of his chauvinistic words, proved to be very handy at helping the work along.

Lory looked at her watch. 'It's nearly eleven,' she said. 'I wonder where Grant is?' He had not of course told her where he was going when he left her—not that she expected it.

'Ach, you know how it is when he gets playing chess with Finlay,' said Jean, looking at Iain. 'Had you better go and fetch him? We all have an early start in the morning.'

'I can walk that way,' answered Lory. 'As long as that's where he is.'

'Will I walk with you?' suggested Iain.

'Oh no, it's a fine clear night.'

'And there are no villains on Creagdubh,' laughed Jean.

'Well, I'd really better be going, then,' said Lory, 'or else I won't be up. I've enjoyed this evening very much.'

They stood in the doorway to wave her off, and she looked back once, and saw them silhouetted in the warm light from the oil lamp, Iain's arm round Jean, she leaning on his shoulder, the two of them looking so utterly right that it gave Lory a pang. How happy they looked. Not much money, a large family, yet with a sense of contentment about them that spread out to warm her when she was with them.

She concentrated on the path ahead, heard the door close in the distance, and went down towards Finlay's house. Through the silent village, everyone abed, and a solitary gleam of light from the end house, Finlay's, outside which Grant's Range-Rover was parked. The moon was high to light her way, nearly full—and she remembered the legend of the Moon-dancers, and knew that she at least would never see them, for soon she would be leaving the island for ever, before it was too late.

She reached the house, intending to knock at the door, then stopped by the gleam from the window and looked in. The scene that met her eyes was to be etched for ever on her brain. The two men sat at a table by the fire, Grant with his back to the window, Finlay facing it. Both appeared engrossed in the chessboard between them, although of course that was an illusion, for Finlay could not see the board. He would rely on his memory, and what Grant told him. That was what Iain had said. That Finlay would know every square on the board, and play by touch—and remember his, and his opponent's, every move so that he would play as well as one with sight.

On the mantelpiece an oil lamp cast a warm glow of light

155

around the two men, and Finlay's dog slept by her master's feet. Lory looked at the back of Grant's head, saw his dark hair touching the neck of his sweater, saw the way it curled at the ends, and wondered, absurdly, if he cut it himself. There was no barber on Creagdubh, she knew that. And then, quite suddenly, almost as if she had called him, he looked round, looked straight at the window, and his eyes met hers. Feeling as foolish as if she had been caught eavesdropping, Lory moved away to the door and knocked hard.

'Come away in.' Grant opened the door to the hall and looked down at her.

'I—I—paused by the window,' she stammered, feeling the need to explain.

'Aye, well, we forgot the time, did we not, Finlay?'

'That is so. Ach, but we had best finish now, eh, Grant, and put the board away.'

'Oh, please don't—I mean——'

'Ach, we can finish it another day. We have all the time in the world.'

All the time in the world. All the time in the world. The words had a music to them that stayed in Lory's head as she waited for Grant to put the chessboard in a safe place at the back of the sideboard where it would remain until they could finish their game. And when they did—she might well have left Creagdubh for ever. For she had not all the time in the world, just another few days...

'Ready, Lory?'

'Yes, I'm ready. Good night, Finlay. I'll visit you again before'—she had been about to say 'before I go,' and altered it to—'before long,' for she didn't want anyone to know. Not yet.

'Ach, I'll see you in the morning, on the boat,' he answered. 'Let us pray for a fine day.'

'Yes. It makes all the difference,' said Grant, and looked at her as if he had noticed the hesitation, almost as if he *knew*. But he couldn't, of course, could he? She had only recently decided herself, and the reason for her decision was something he could *never* guess, not in a million years.

'Did you have a pleasant evening at Iain's?' he asked as they set off in the Range-Rover. His tone implied that he didn't care, not at all, and she felt the familiar tightening of her lips at his manner. He had the power to infuriate her even without speaking, so how much worse it was when he did. The sooner she got away from him, the better.

'Very pleasant, thank you. Iain is very nice. And very funny. You're good friends, are you?' and she managed to inject a note of surprise in the last question, very subtly, of course, for she had experience of his sarcasm, but she couldn't resist it even so.

'And you wonder why?' No subtlety there, merely a blunt question.

She took a deep breath. Why, oh, why don't I keep my mouth shut? she thought. 'I would think *he*'s a friendly person,' she answered.

And Grant began to laugh. 'That's not what you mean at all,' he said. 'True he is, but you really mean—why the hell would he want a man like me as his friend? You'll never understand that, little Miss Brains, and I don't intend to waste my time telling you.' They were driving along the moonlit track at a moderate speed, and he began to whistle softly, as if dismissing her completely from his mind.

Oh, I could hit him, thought Lory. I really could. He is infuriating, arrogant, *hateful*—especially to *me*—and I wonder, that being so, why on earth I should find that not only can't I get him out of my mind, but—and she gritted her teeth. No! she thought. No. I will not even think it. I will not. For as long as she didn't admit it to herself, she would be safe. She hoped.

Dreams which were so vivid and disturbing that they woke her several times, dreams which trailed away into shadows that left her confused and uncertain—and a last, particularly clear dream in which Grant came into her room, knelt by her bed, and asked her to marry him and live on Creagdubh—and from this she woke filled with warmth and love—and saw Grant standing by the bed.

Instantly the warmth vanished with the images of the dream, shattered into a thousand fragments by the hard reality of his presence as he said softly:

'It is half past six, Lory. Time to get up. I have brought you a cup of tea. Breakfast in the kitchen as soon as you are ready.'

'Mmm. Thank you.' Disorientated, not fully awake—or aware—she just wanted him to go.

'You won't go back to sleep? We must leave within half an hour for the Campbells.'

And that sobered her sufficiently to bid farewell to the last tattered remnants of sleep. She sat up. 'Not now,' she answered. 'I'll be down in ten minutes. That's a promise.'

He turned and went out as silently as he had come in, closing the door after him. Lory drank the hot strong tea and felt it clearing her mind. What dreams she had had! All now only vaguely remembered, save the last which was too fresh to vanish. And that had been too ridiculous for words, and she really would try and forget it as soon as possible.

She felt better after a wash and cleaning her teeth, and dressed quickly, slipping two seasickness pills into her pocket before going down the stairs, coat and bag over her arm.

The kitchen was warm, and Grant was already tucking into bacon and eggs. He looked up, and before he could speak, Lory said: 'Just toast for me, please—I would have said when you brought the tea, but I wasn't awake properly.'

He nodded. 'As you wish. Are you sure?'

'Quite sure, thank you.' Then, as he made to get up: 'I'll do it. Please finish yours.' She went to the stove and put two slices of bread under the grill to save further discussion.

Ten minutes later they were on their way to the Campbells' house. She wondered what he was thinking. Was he worried in case Mrs. Campbell had a last-minute panic and refused to go? He didn't appear to have anything else on his mind except the concentration needed to drive along the bumpy and rather misty track. She stole a sidelong glance at him. He wore his kilt, and a dark blue rollnecked sweater, and grey knee-length socks, and sturdy black shoes, and he looked—she had to swallow before even admitting it to herself—he looked devastatingly attractive. Of course, she reasoned to herself, she didn't often see kilted men in the London streets, and so it was just unusual, that was all. But it wasn't all; it was more than that. Far more. He was powerfully built, a big man without a spare ounce of fat on him, muscular, with a character as tough as his appearance and that unsuspected streak of gentleness that is said to be possessed by all truly strong men. For he was kind, she knew that, and couldn't even deny it to herself. She had seen it the previous night when she had watched him playing chess with Finlay; she had seen it when he was with Jean's children—and she had seen it with Mrs. Campbell, and surely would again, very soon, for they were nearly there.

'Help me,' she said, and she knew it was an odd thing to say, and wasn't even sure why she had done so, even when the words were out. But he didn't ask why, he didn't even look puzzled. He merely answered, very quietly:

'I will. It may be easier than you think. She may just need something like this—or someone like you—to break her out of her long solitude.'

'Yes. But I feel—it's such a big responsibility. I offered, and I didn't know *why*.'

'You, a sociologist, didn't know *why* you'd done something?' But his words were only gently mocking, not unkind, and she sensed that he was, in a way, helping her already. The truce, it seemed, was on again.

She laughed. 'All right, perhaps I did. I wanted to help her.'

'And that is reason enough, surely?'

'Of course. I suppose I just need reassurance that I'm doing the right thing. She's been at home so long. Perhaps she's happier that way——'

'No!' His answer was vehement. 'No, she needs company—only she doesn't realize it. You have given her the chance. We mustn't fail.'

He had said 'we.' We mustn't fail. She wasn't on her own in this. And she had the villagers behind her too. But Grant—it was he who counted most. A warm glow suffused her very being. We must not fail. And it was then that she knew that they wouldn't.

The boat was a large one—as it needed to be, for there were over thirty villagers on it, and the atmosphere was festive and happy. Lory had very discreetly taken her seasickness pill before they set off, and was ready to face the unknown voyage with a certain calm. She sat on deck with Mr. and Mrs. Campbell and Grant, and could almost feel the tangible waves of well-being surrounding them from the other passengers, although everyone was keeping a tactful distance. All had greeted the little grey woman, some with shy nods, some with a smile and a word, and now she sat clutching a large bag on her knee as if it were her defence against the world, but already there was a subtle change in her, almost an awakening, as she looked out over the water and saw Creagdubh dwindle to a smudge on the horizon. Her husband had his arm round her, and the talk was of the games, and of Grant's part in them, and a little smile touched her mouth as Grant said something funny.

It's going to be all right, Lory thought. It is. She caught Grant's eye and knew that the same thought was in his mind. He crouched down in front of Mrs. Campbell.

'I'm away to the galley,' he said. 'Will you have tea or coffee?'

She looked startled, as if he might be leaving for good, and John Campbell squeezed her waist protectively. 'Tea, please, Grant,' she said.

'Aye. Good and hot and sweet.' He grinned at them all, turned and strode across the deck to the steps leading down to the cabin. Jean and her children, and the other village children were there where they could be safely under supervision with no chance of one slipping overboard.

The sun was strong, and the air was fresh and cold and salty-tasting to the lips, and Lory felt a sudden surge of happiness and well-being. Impulsively, she leaned across and spoke to Mrs Campbell. 'I'm so glad you've come today,' she said. 'Truly glad. It's going to be a good day, I feel it in my bones.'

Mrs. Campbell looked at her, and then she smiled. 'Aye, it is,' she agreed. 'All thanks to you.'

'No thanks to me,' Lory answered. 'I didn't arrange this voyage, I'm just a passenger like you. Oh, it's all so new to me—I'm so looking forward to the games. I've brought my camera as well. I hope I can take lots of photos.' And silently she added to herself—and some snaps of Grant. And she knew why, but she wasn't going to admit it even to herself.

'Och, you'll be able to do that fine. It's all colour there—and noise, though you cannot capture that on film, alas, but you will recall it all when you see the photos.'

'And I'll send you some if they turn out all right, shall I?' Lory smiled.

'That would be nice. You are kind, Lory.'

And then Grant returned with a huge jug of tea, and several beakers, and the next few minutes were occupied with seeing that none was spilt as it was transferred. And Lory was able to look around her at the other passengers, and it was a strangely heartening feeling to realize that she knew them all, in varying degrees. Finlay—Sister Grant—

161

the Macdonalds—the little postmistress, sitting talking to another village woman Lory had spoken to only briefly—Iain busy at the controls way up on the bridge—even the Macleods were there, and had waved to her as they all embarked on Creagdubh. She knew she was not one of them, and would soon be away, but she knew too that she would never forget any of them, not as long as she lived.

Then she heard it, the growing murmur, and she looked ahead at the pointing arms, and saw the smudge of land ahead, and her pulses leapt. Grant, looking up from his beaker of tea, met her eyes with his own, and smiled. 'Aye,' he said. 'That's it, we're nearly there now.' He stood up and called out, 'And we're going to beat them at everything, are we not?'

A full-throated roar of agreement went up, mingled with laughter, and from the bridge came the deep hoot of the boat's siren as Iain added his own approval of the statement. Then Grant moved away, and signalled two of the men, and vanished with them. And John Campbell, the other side of his wife, began to chuckle. 'Better to get your camera out now, lassie,' he said. 'For you are about to see a sight you will not forget in a hurry.'

Lory leant forward, the better to see his face. 'What?' she asked.

'Wait and see. Wait and see.' He was grinning broadly. There was even a sparkle of curiosity in his wife's eyes. And they waited, as in the distance the island they were to visit drew even nearer, becoming clearer each moment.

Then Lory heard the sounds, and that trickle of surprise and delight touched her spine. The sound of bagpipes, still faint, but gathering strength every second, and then the three men appeared from the other side of the bridge, giving their all with 'Scotland the Brave,' three marching kilted men with Grant as their leader, and she bent to her bag for her camera, and wondered why her hands should be trembling so, why the music had such power to disturb and excite her.

The murmur of the others rose to a chorus as they all joined in singing an accompaniment to the music as she raised her camera to photograph them.

And that was how they arrived at the games, piped on shore by their laird, Grant Mackinnon, the man they all loved, and would follow anywhere, a cheerful, laughing crowd of islanders who were greeted at the jetty by their hosts. This, thought Lory, is a day I shall always remember. Which turned out to be true in a way she could not possibly have foreseen.

CHAPTER ELEVEN

THE hammer throwing was in progress, and Lory sat with Jean and her children, and Mr. and Mrs. Campbell, in a little group at the side of the field, and it seemed quite natural that they should all be together, although she wasn't quite sure herself how it had come about, except that Donald, Jean's youngest boy, had attached himself very firmly to Mrs. Campbell from the moment they had arrived, and was now sitting comfortably asleep on her knee. Lory felt that if anyone spoke about it, the magic might go away, that the whole scene was like a fragile web spun in gold, that it was *right*.

Jean's mother had been at school with Mrs. Campbell. Perhaps it was a link that enabled the little woman to speak. Whatever the reason, Lory uttered a silent prayer of thanks. And Jean was just perfect. She had not pushed too much, or offered friendship in a way that might frighten the timid woman back into her shell. She had offered sandwiches, and they had been accepted, and John Campbell had been away to the large tent for jugs of tea, and milk for the children, and everything was going far better than Lory had hoped.

It was Grant and Iain now in the final with two of the opposing islanders, and excitement mounted. Lory stood up, camera at the ready, and raised it to her eyes as Grant prepared for the final throw. His sweater was off, he stood there, tall and still, waiting for silence, in command of the situation, kilted, stripped to the waist, as were all the other men, and his body was very muscular and powerful. Click! another photograph. Then she waited, ready to take one of him in action, knowing it might be blurred but prepared to risk it. Jean looked up from hushing the children and said, smiling: 'You'll maybe take one of Iain as well, for a souvenir?'

'Oh, of course!' answered Lory. 'I'm snapping as much as I can of *everyone*.'

She emphasized the last word to cover her own uneasy guilt at the knowledge that so far she had managed to get at least ten shots of Grant in various activities and not quite the same number of everything else combined. She had two more rolls of film in her bag, and hoped that no one had actually been counting. Jean seemed to be enjoying herself immensely, as did everyone else, but Lory had a faint suspicion that she was more observant than the rest. Just in case she did think anything, Lory turned away from Grant and snapped their own little group, the children dancing up and down as they waved to their father, Mrs. Campbell holding the sleeping child, her husband stacking paper cups tidily away, Jean looking up and smiling, as if she knew precisely what was in Lory's mind. Lory smiled at her in return. She had an ally there, a friend, and if she guessed, what did it matter? Somehow she would not mind Jean knowing all there was to know, and it was precious little anyway. For what more was there than the one basic fact? She, Lory Stevenson, free, white and over twenty-one, had had the misfortune to find herself in love for the first time in her life, and with a man who regarded her as rather a nuisance, to put it at its most charitable—Grant Mackinnon, Laird of Creagdubh. And in a few days she would have to go away because the knowledge was becoming too painful for her to bear.

'I could do with a wee walk,' said Jean suddenly. 'All this sitting down is doing me no good.' She pulled an apologetic face at Mrs. Campbell. 'Would you——' she began.

'Aye. Off you go. I'll watch the bairns.'

'Thank you. It's just to stretch my legs.' Mr. Campbell

and Lory helped her to her feet, and they set off walking away from the field and the crowd of people dotted round.

'What about the photo of Iain?' protested Lory.

'Och, I was only teasing. Who needs a photo of him? I have him all the time.'

'You know, don't you?' asked Lory quietly.

'Aye, that I do. Never fear, there's only me can see it. You love Grant, do you not?'

'Yes. And I can tell you now, I'm going home next week. Tuesday is it the plane comes?'

'Yes. But your work, Lory? Surely you are here for three weeks?'

'I've done all I can do. I'm better away.'

'I'll miss you. You know that? I'll really miss you. We must write to each other.'

'Of course we will. And I'll soon manage to forget—him.'

'Och, of course. You'll have no shortage of boy-friends.'

'No,' agreed Lory. No, I won't, she thought, but there'll be no one could ever be like him.

They strolled round the perimeter of the field, and it was pleasant, with the sun shining, the large flat field with refreshment tent at one end, the places marked off for various activities, the two lots of islanders mingling to exchange gossip and news, the distant view of the village, and beyond it the sea, and further away still, over the horizon, Creagdubh, Lory's magic island, the place she would never forget.

She sighed. It was time to change the subject. 'Mrs. Campbell is just fine, isn't she?' she asked. 'Although Donald has helped—we couldn't have done better if we'd arranged it, could we?'

Jean laughed. 'Couldn't we? Do you think you're the only one who gets bright ideas round here?'

'W—what do you mean?' There was something in Jean's voice . . .

'I told him she was a sort of granny, and that if he was

kind to her he would get a nice surprise when he got home. He's a bright wee laddie, is my Donald.'

'Oh, Jean! You're marvellous!' Lory began to laugh. 'How can I thank you?'

'Och, what for? It's you that's done it all so far. But for you she would not be here today, and that's a fact. I've just helped a little, that's all. Besides, she was a school friend of my mother's, and they both went to be nurses when they were old enough. My mum is dead now, but I know she would have wanted me to do what I could, for they were close.'

'Mrs. Campbell was a nurse?' Lory was startled, although with no reason.

'Aye, and a good one by all accounts. Och, it's fine to see her again, and if it lasts, and there's no reason it shouldn't, she'll join in village life again. Oh, Lory, you should be here in winter when we have the *ceilidhs*, the gatherings. You would like them.'

'I'm sure I would. Finlay was telling me, and the Macdonalds. They all seem to be having a good time here today, don't they?'

'Everyone does. And when the weather is this—aah!' she clutched Lory's arm, and stopped walking.

'Jean? What is it?' Lory saw, in alarm, that the other's face had gone white.

Jean took a few deep breaths. 'Nothing. It's gone now.' She closed her eyes. 'That's better. Just a twinge. Probably the baby kicking. I knew I was sat too long.'

'Are you sure?' persisted Lory.

'Yes.' Jean stared at her levelly. 'And you are not to say anything. Not even to Iain. He'll only get in a fuss, and the day is not over. I'll be fine.' She put her arm in Lory's and laughed. 'Och, dinna fuss so much! It's me having the bairn, not you. Now, let's get back to the others, and remember—not a word.'

But it was obvious on the return journey that Jean was not

fine at all. Lory and Mrs. Campbell and Sister Grant stayed in the cabin with her after Iain had carried her on to the boat, torn between concern and the desire to scold her for keeping so quiet when she was so clearly in distress.

The children were being looked after by Mr. Campbell and Grant on deck, while Iain kept full speed back to Creagdubh. Betty Grant was calmness itself, sitting beside Jean, who lay on a bunk covered by a blanket.

'We'll soon have you home,' she said soothingly. 'And then we'll have things sorted out in no time.'

'The baby's coming, I know that,' answered Jean. She was very white, but managing to smile. 'And I'm not having it anywhere else but in my own home, d'you see?'

'Ach, I know that,' laughed the nurse. 'And you will. It's a few hours off yet. The little fellow's impatient, that's all. He cannot wait a couple more weeks, but he can wait a few more hours, never fear.'

'I know. You'll not leave me, Sister?'

'I won't leave you——' She turned at an urgent knock from the door to the cabin. 'Tell them everything's all right, Lory, will you?'

Lory opened the door, expecting to see Grant or Iain enquiring after his wife, but it was the little postmistress, Miss Carmichael, eyes wide with concern.

'Can the Sister come quickly?' she whispered. 'There's two of them are ill—something they ate, we think—och, but they're awful sick!'

Betty Grant patted Jean's hand. 'Aye well, things come in threes, don't they? At least they're not expecting! I'll not be a minute, love. Keep an eye on her, Mrs. Campbell.'

She went quickly out. Lory looked at Mrs. Campbell helplessly. The little woman sat on the edge of Jean's bunk. 'There now,' she said. 'Perhaps it's just as well I came today,' and she smiled. 'You never really forget being a nurse, even though it's a long while ago. It's like swimming or riding a bike.'

She had changed. It was unbelievable, but it was so. This

calm woman sitting there was completely different from the grey mouselike creature who had so timidly greeted Lory only days previously in her home.

'I'm glad we brought our own sandwiches,' said Jean, with a brave attempt at a smile. 'I don't fancy food poisoning on top of everything else. I wonder what it could have been?'

'Och, too much drink, perhaps,' answered Mrs. Campbell. 'For didn't John himself tell me he'd seen some supping whisky behind the tent?'

But it was not that, for when Sister Grant came back it was to say that there were now six villagers feeling distinctly under the weather—and they had all been eating the same meat paste sandwiches from the tent. 'And that's not the worst of it,' she added. 'I had some as well. I've given everyone who ate them—and myself—a good dose of medicine—and now I'll just have to keep my fingers crossed. Did any of you eat anything from the refreshment tent?'

Lory answered. 'We all had sandwiches that we made at Jean's last night.'

'Thank God,' breathed Betty Grant. 'Look, Jean love, I'd better not go any nearer to you. I've just scrubbed my hands with antiseptic, but I can't chance passing any infection on——' she stopped. She looked a little pale herself, but was clearly a woman of immense reserves of will power.

Then Mrs. Campbell spoke. Her voice was quiet but it carried such authority that Lory felt her spine tingle at it. 'You need not worry, Sister,' she said. 'I can look after Jean.'

There was a moment's silence as the nurse and Mrs. Campbell exchanged glances. Then Betty Grant nodded. 'Aye,' she said, 'I know you can. And you may have to. And you, Lory?'

'I'll do anything you want me to,' answered Lory.

'You seem to forget me,' said Jean plaintively. 'Don't

you think, with my brood, I'm capable of delivering myself if necessary?' Her remark lightened the tension in the room immediately. Betty Grant smiled.

'That's the spirit,' she said. 'Now, I must go and see if anyone else needs me. You have only to call. I'll hear you, and I'll come.' And with that, she went out.

Jean dozed off, clearly unworried now that she was on her way home. Lory went to look out through the tiny porthole at the calm sea. With all the excitement she had forgotten her second seasickness pill—and she wasn't even slightly perturbed. There were far more important things on her mind.

She sat quietly on the other bunk, and waited for the journey to end. In her mind came a kaleidoscope of the day's events, colourful, exciting—the races, the bagpipe contest—won by Grant—the hammer throwing, caber tossing—won by Iain—everything a bright whirl of memory she would be able to take out and savour as if from some mental photographic album, whenever she wished. She would not have wanted to miss this day for the world. But it hadn't finished yet.

It was clear by the time they reached Creagdubh that Sister Grant would not be able to be of much help. It was equally clear that Jean's baby was going to arrive very shortly.

Lory touched Mrs. Campbell's hand as Iain helped Jean from her bunk. 'We're in this together,' she said softly. She felt her own hand grasped in return.

'And I could not wish for a better one to help me,' the little woman whispered. 'You have changed my life for me today, in a way you cannot imagine. I owe you a lot for that.'

'You owe me nothing. I'm frightened——'

'Why?'

'Because I don't know the first thing about babies being born—only what I've seen on television——'

'You've seen things like *that* on the television?' Mrs.

Campbell's eyes widened in greatest surprise. 'Whatever next?'

Lory laughed, and impulsively hugged her. 'You're marvellous!' she said. 'Come on, let's help Iain.' And together they followed them out of the cabin.

It was evening now, with a soft cool light to the air, and those villagers who were fit were assisting their stricken neighbours to their homes. Most were recovering rapidly; although it was clear the stomach upset was not a serious one, nevertheless, it was unpleasant enough to leave them rather shaky-legged, and Sister Grant came over to the little group as they made their way off the boat.

'I will be up to the house as soon as I can,' she said, 'to help by remote control, as it were. Don't worry about your children, Jean, they are going to the Macleods for the night.' She was very pale herself.

'You mustn't worry about *me*,' Jean answered. 'I don't know what all the fuss is about, it's only a ba——' she stopped and drew in breath sharply.

'Off you go.' Sister Grant nodded to Iain. 'No sense in giving birth here when you'd be more comfortable in bed.' And she turned away to attend to her other patients.

Iain swung Jean up in his arms, and they went up towards their home. To her surprise, Lory found that she had barely thought about Grant for at least fifteen minutes—when he ran up behind them.

'Everything all right, Iain?' he called.

'Aye. Away and attend to your business,' was the reply. Lory turned round and, resisting the temptation to stick her tongue out at him, said:

'We'll manage, Grant, thank you, Mrs. Campbell and I.'

His glance was hard and level—and with something in it that made her legs turn to jelly. 'I know you will. Mrs. Campbell, John has gone back with Finlay and will wait at his house for you.'

'Aye, well, he may have a long wait, tell him,' she re-

171

plied, this new woman that nobody had ever really seen before. 'Because I'll not be leaving Jean's until the bairn is safely arrived, and we don't know when that will be, do we?'

'I'll away and tell him.'

'Yes, you do that,' said Lory sweetly, taking Mrs. Campbell's arm, and giving a final glance at Grant before she turned away. In an odd way she felt almost sorry for him. For the first time since she had met him, he didn't look entirely in command of the situation. It was quite a satisfying knowledge to have.

With Jean safely tucked up in bed, Lory made a pot of tea for them all and they sat drinking it in the bedroom. The crib was ready. All they had to do now, it seemed, was wait for the baby's arrival. Iain had departed to the Sister's house to see if she was fit to come, which Lory fervently hoped she would be—although Mrs. Campbell seemed to be the least concerned of the three. The change in her was really quite amazing, and Lory could only marvel at it.

And then, quite quickly, it was all over. Jean gave a cry, Mrs. Campbell said urgently: 'The blankets—quickly, Lory——' and the miracle happened.

A tiny red creature, squalling lustily, assisted by Mrs. Campbell's skilful hands, emerged into the world. Lory held tightly to Jean's hand, soothing her as she witnessed the most wonderful sight of all. In five minutes it was all over. Jean lay back, propped up on three pillows, nursing her newest daughter in her arms and looking very proud of herself as well she might, while Mrs. Campbell and Lory cleared everything tidily away ready for visitors.

'But I can't get over it,' Lory said, still slightly dazed at the speed of it all. 'I thought we'd be there for hours—I mean—you know, labour and everything——' They were in the kitchen of the house.

Mrs. Campbell laughed. 'After all those bairns? Och no, maybe for the first, but with the ones she's had, why, it's like shelling peas. She must have known on the boat that it wouldna' be long, but she was determined to be in her own bed, you see.'

'And you were marvellous,' exclaimed Lory. 'What would we have done without you?'

'Och, you'd have managed all right,' but she smiled as she said it, and looked pleased all the same. 'Now, away and take this cup of tea to Jean. The poor lass could do with it, while I warm up this soup for us.'

Back in the bedroom Lory put the tightly wrapped bundle in her cot while Jean sipped the hot tea. 'I'm tired, Lory,' she said. 'But before I go to sleep will you let me have a little talk alone with Mrs. Campbell? I want to make sure that we don't let her retire into her shell again. I'm going to ask her to visit us regularly after you've gone, for you'll not be here much longer, will you—and I'd like to keep up the good work you started.'

'Of course! That will be perfect. I was hoping you'd be able to do something—in fact I was going to ask you, when you'd rested, of course——'

'Aye, well, I'll do it now—when she wouldn't refuse, and especially if I tell her Donald—and all the others—need a granny. Don't worry, Lory, your good efforts won't be wasted now.'

'I'll send her up.' She could see Jean was tired, and went quickly down the stairs. 'I'll watch the soup,' she told Mrs. Campbell. 'I think Jean wants a word with you.' She crossed her fingers in childish superstition as she waited by the pan. But she already knew everything was going to be all right. At least some good would come of her journey to Creagdubh. As for me, she thought wryly, I've made a mess of things and no mistake—but there's an old saying that covers it: put it down to experience. She managed to grab the pan just in time before the hot broth bubbled over.

It was very late, past midnight and already Sunday. Mr. and Mrs. Campbell, Grant, Iain and Lory were sitting

173

round the large table in the living room. There was an almost empty bottle on the table, and glasses in front of each of them. Although they spoke quietly, in deference to the Sabbath, the atmosphere was festive. Jean was soundly asleep with her daughter upstairs, and in a way it was for all of them as if they had come to the end of a long hard working day and were enjoying a well-earned rest from their labours. But there was more; there was a sense of achievement shared. And in this both Lory and Mrs. Campbell had played a major part.

Iain's gratitude was genuine and almost overwhelming. He had returned with written instructions from Sister Grant to find that they really weren't needed. Lory had many memories of Creagdubh, but now one of the most outstanding would be the sight of Iain as he walked softly to his wife's bed, knelt by her side, and took her in his arms. No words were needed. Lory had walked quietly from the room unnoticed. There had been a lump in her throat.

Grant had been waiting in the living room. Waiting and watching. And he had seen her face. Lory had tilted her chin. What did it matter? She would soon be free of him. Free and away, no longer having to wonder about him, to do battle with him—to look at him with pain in her heart, and the knowledge that she loved him in a hopeless way. Then he had spoken.

'So you have done a grand job tonight, haven't you?' he had said quietly.

'Mrs. Campbell did. I helped,' she had answered. Oh, why didn't he go away?

'Aye, both of you. Iain won't forget.' Mrs. Campbell was in another room ironing. She had insisted that she enjoyed it, and would not be talked out of it.

'As long as Mrs. Campbell keeps coming here, as she has agreed to do, that's all the thanks I need,' she had answered.

Lory thought back on the scene now as she listened to the

174

conversation flowing around her. Grant and Iain, sitting side by side, were like two brothers. Lory, in spite of her remarks to Grant about their friendship, could see that there was a bond of affection between them that was heartening to see. It was like being in another world. This close-knit community had a spirit of its own. She had seen it more than ever in the past few hours, when those unfortunates who had eaten the wrong sandwiches had been taken into their homes to be cared for by neighbours; when Mr. and Mrs. Macleod had taken Jean's children to their schoolhouse to be looked after, and Grant had been busily occupied in visiting everyone to ensure no one had been missed. Miss Carmichael had opened her shop for all who needed medicine, 'just in case,' and Grant had reappeared at Iain's eventually with an unlabelled bottle, and the injunction: 'Ask no questions,' the reason for which Lory realized when she began to drink the deceptively mild-looking gold liquid.

She had spluttered as the first golden sip went down. 'It's—it's very strong,' she had managed, to the sound of the others' laughter.

'Aye, that it is,' said John Campbell. 'A good wee bit stronger than the stuff ye'll buy in the shops, eh, Grant?' He had looked blandly innocent.

'Is that a fact? Aye, well, drink up.'

'Is it——' Lory hardly dared ask. 'Is it home-made whisky?'

'But that would be illegal!' Mrs. Campbell answered. 'And we're none of us lawbreakers, eh, Grant?'

'Indeed not! What an idea. Let's just say it's some that a friend found buried in a cupboard.' And he had lifted his glass. 'Here's to you, Iain, and your new bairn. Drink up, everyone!'

Now the bottle was nearly empty, and Lory found to her dismay that she was extremely tired. Mrs. Campbell saw her face and stood up, and looked at Grant. 'Had you better be getting Lory home?' she suggested. 'She's had a busy day.'

'But I——' protested Lory. 'I thought I might stay—in case Jean needed anything.'

'Ach, I'll stay, child. Away you go to your bed now. I'll make a pot of tea to see you on your way. Iain will find me a bed, I'm sure.'

'Only too happy, Mrs. Campbell. In fact you can all stay if you want—there's room enough now the children are away.'

The kettle bubbled on the fire, and tea was brewed, and whisky added to it—'so that we can bury the bottle,' said Iain with a wink at Grant.

Lory blinked, wondering why the room seemed to be getting more blurred every minute. Strange, that. She knew she was tired, but surely she hadn't had enough whisky to affect her. She sipped her tea, and that didn't help much. In fact she longed just to put her head down on the table and go to sleep, which would, of course, be incredibly bad-mannered. But the temptation was almost irresistible.

'Come away, Lory.' A gentle hand was on her shoulder, and she realized to her horror that her eyes had been closed. It was Grant.

Good nights were said, and they went out to the Range-Rover, and once inside it, Lory closed her eyes and went to sleep.

The plans were made, and she would not change them. It was Sunday evening, and Lory sat in her room sorting through her notes, going through her mental list of tasks for the following day, Monday, which would be her final one on Creagdubh. A visit to the Macleods to return the book on the Moon-dancers, a visit to Finlay—and one to Jean, the last visit of all. There would be no opportunity to visit the Campbells or Macdonalds because they were too far, but she would leave a note for Mrs. Campbell at Jean's. A quick call in to the nurse to see how she was, and then she would be ready to leave.

And on Tuesday she would be on the plane, and away. Away for good. Only Jean knew, and that was the way Lory wanted it. She had intended avoiding Grant as much as possible—but it hadn't been necessary, for she hadn't even seen him once during the entire day. It had given her time to think about the games on Saturday, and the even more exciting events afterwards—and while at the moment they still tended to be one glorious colourful blur, one fact seemed to be emerging in painful clarity. It was not her imagination. From the very start of the day, Grant had been a different man. There had been the small truce before they reached the Campbells'—but after that, it had been as though there were a barrier between them. Invisible to others, certainly, for both of them had been determined to make Mrs. Campbell feel at ease as much as possible, but there all the same.

Lory put her chin in her hands. Confess it, she said to herself, for a sociologist who doesn't do so badly at communicating with people, you're just one heck of a mixed-up creature yourself. All right, I admit it, she thought. What am I supposed to do about it? Fling my arms round him and tell him I'm crazy about him? Oh yes, that *would* be hilarious!

'Damn!' Several papers fluttered to the floor and she bent to pick them up. A solitary tear trickled down her face and plopped on to the top sheet, and she looked out of the window to see her own face reflected in the glass, for it had gone dark, very dark, with low threatening clouds scurrying across the sky, and she had had to put her light on. She stood up and went to switch it off, then returned to the window to look out. A wave of overwhelming sadness engulfed her. This place, this stark, beautiful island was not her home, and soon—too soon—she would leave it, but it had a place in her heart just as surely as its laird had. And life would probably never be the same again. Never.

It was no use. She would have to have a walk before

bedtime or she would never sleep. It wasn't raining, but it soon could be, and there would be no more soaking wet hair, or borrowed hair dryers. Lory took out her mackintosh, rain hat, and for good measure, her telescopic umbrella. Thus armed, she slipped on her coat and left the room.

She bumped into Edna on the way down. 'Not going out, dear?' the friendly woman enquired. 'It's going to pour down.'

Lory smiled and held up her umbrella. 'I know,' she answered, 'but I'm prepared. I've had a bit of a headache all day—that will clear it.'

'Mind how you go, love, and don't forget—coffee in half an hour.'

'I'll remember. 'Bye, Edna.'

She stood indecisively for a moment or two on the front steps, then set off, destination decided, for one last look at the bird sanctuary.

She put her mackintosh on after a short while, not because it had begun raining, but because a strong wind had blown up, and it was colder than she had imagined it would be. Her hair was blown about wildly as she toiled up the hill towards the cliff, from where—if it wasn't too dark—she would see the island that Grant had taken her to. Above the wind she could hear the roaring of the sea as it dashed against the rocks, and she shivered. It was all very well to watch scenes on television from the comfort of an easy chair, and reflect how stormy and romantic it all was, but the reality was vastly different. It was exciting, stirring to the blood, but it was leg-aching, struggling to walk, and the wind bit into her bones, and froze her face so that it ached, and the sound of it all was in her ears like a wild chorus, deafening her to anything else, filling her head with the tumultuous fancies that here, in this remote place, anything could happen. There could be magic in the very air—but not the Moon-dancers, that was sure, for the moon was well

178

hidden behind black, lowering clouds, and would not re-appear until they had gone. She almost wished for rain, because even that would not be as cold as this cruel, biting wind, and she raised her face to the sky, and then stumbled slightly, because unless you watched every inch of the way it could be dangerous.

She was nearly there now. Nearly at the cliff top, and she had no intention of going too near. That first nightmare vision of Grant simply vanishing over the side, down the hidden path, was too vivid. All her memories of Creagdubh were vivid. Could she ever have imagined it would be *dull*? A choked laugh escaped her, and was whipped away by the wind.

Lory pulled her mac tighter round her and slowed her walk. Carefully now, visions of a sudden gust of wind tear-ing her over the edge making her steps cautious and halting. She looked out to sea. She stood alone, a slender solitary figure outlined against blackish sky and cloud, hair blowing about her face, cheeks tingling with the cold; stood still, quite still, and breathed of the air that tasted of salt and heather and the thousand other things that went to make Creagdubh what it was. Her mind was soothed, because in this very wildness was a kind of emotional calm. If I can withstand this, she thought, I can withstand anything, even loving a man to whom I am nothing.

And as she raised her face to the sky, the first drops of rain fell upon it. Deceptively soft, for they were followed, almost immediately, by a tumultuous downpour of such force that she gasped, fumbling for her rain-hat—the umbrella would be blown inside out in seconds—and as she reached up to put her hat on, three things happened with startling suddenness.

A blinding flash of lightning lit the entire sky with bril-liant yellow, to be followed almost immediately by the roar of thunder, shaking the ground beneath her—and the wind whipped her hat from her grasp. Blinded, frightened, she reached out, but her sense of direction had gone, because she could scarcely see, only the dazzling blue whirls in her eyes—and she stumbled—and the cliff edge crumbled away beneath her feet in one terrifying moment.

Down, down, in agony, screaming, falling, seeing quite unrelated events flashing in front of her eyes in tantalizing panorama—her father's face—the birth of Jean's baby—a pet dog she had had as a child—and the thought of death, because she knew she was going to die—and then—nothing.

Lory opened her eyes. Distantly came a roll of thunder, reverberating round the heavens, and she wondered if this was what had roused her. She didn't know where she was, or what had happened, only that she hurt all over, and didn't want to move. All she could see was a black sky, and even that was blurred, for the rain fell on her upturned face with an undiminished vigour and she was cold, oh, so very cold. But she was alive. And she began to remember what had happened on the cliff top. There had been lightning—a crash of thunder, and she had felt herself falling. So she must be on the beach. She managed to turn her head slightly, and the sea was very close, wildly dashing against nearby rocks, looking, from the angle at which she lay, as if it might overwhelm her at any minute.

'The cave,' she mouthed. 'I must get to the cave.' But the effort was too great even to think about, and her head fell back on to soft springy heather. She remembered, vaguely, the large clump near the bottom of the track down. It must have been that which had broken her fall. After a minute— or it might have been an hour, she no longer had any sensation of time passing, she roused herself to make the supreme effort to actually move. First her hands, flexing each finger carefully, then her arms, raising each one cautiously, an inch at a time. She could do it. There was a small feeling of triumph at this achievement. Then, carefully, she moved her right leg, ankle first, then calf—but when she attempted to shift her left leg, the sudden startling agony made her cry out. She lay panting for a few seconds trying to quiet the crescendo of utter fear that possessed her. Her leg was broken. It must be. But there was no one else there, only she could help herself. Fearful of what she might discover, Lory attempted to move her back, to sit up. It took what seemed like ages, but she managed it, clawing, grasping, pulling herself up by grabbing at deep-rooted clumps of heather.

There, she was sitting up. Now she was going to crawl to the cave, for shelter. And I'm going to do it now, she told herself. Not in an hour, but now. I *will* do it.

Progress was slow, with each yard costing her much in effort and pain, but she was making it. Safely there, where the storm and rain could not touch her, she would be all right. Further than that she could not, would not, think. She began to count out loud, to take her mind off the pain of her leg. I'll be there before I get to a hundred, she thought, and if I'm not, I'll count again——

'One—two—three——' Her arms ached with the effort, and her body cried out for her to stop, but the counting had become a drum in her ears so that it was all she could hear.

'One hundred and ten—one hundred and eleven——' She was there. The ground was rough and hard and cold, but the rain stopped, and the sound of the sea receded as she dragged herself, inch by agonizing inch, safely away from the open mouth of the cave, to the side, so that she could sit upright, for somewhere deep in her mind was the thought that she must not fall asleep . . .

She opened her eyes, and it was all so quiet now. No wind, no rain, but a clear dark sky with stars, and in the cave, not quite touching her, a thin path of silver moonlight. Lory took a deep breath. She must have slept, but had no awareness of having done so. She looked out towards the sea, and it was calm again, bathed in dazzling white from the moon's glow. Shimmering, dancing with light, sweetly peopled with gauzy insubstantial creatures that waltzed around in never-ending patterns in a gay dance

... Lory blinked, then closed her eyes and counted to ten. If they were still there when she'd finished counting, she would *know* that she was delirious, and she would be frightened; but they wouldn't be, of course.

'Ten.' She opened her eyes, and they were still there, clearer than ever, but she didn't feel feverish, not at all, nor, oddly enough, frightened. Merely curious and so fascinated that she was even able to forget her pain for a few minutes. She took a deep breath. Now, she thought, I've heard about them, and I've read about them, and I know it's all superstition, and I'm quite clear-headed and logical, so I know it's my imagination, just as Grant did, years ago, but even so—— She took a long clear look at the sea, and knew that it was just an illusion of the light. The moon played funny tricks with shadows. Why, she'd been terrified of a rock that had come to life, and had turned out to be a sheep, and all that *this* was were waves being caught by the silver beams and moving——

Moving, gentler now, as if in a waltz, and those were beautiful dresses they had on, long and flowing, white and silver and lacy, and soft, soft, and almost as if there was music——

'Lory! Lory! Are you there?' The loud shout echoed round her, and suddenly there was nothing but moonlight on the sea as Lory called back:

'Yes. Grant—I'm here—in the cave——'

'Thank God,' but that was fainter, and she might have imagined it, and she began to crawl towards the mouth of the cave, in case she had to shout out again, in case he would go away.

'Stay there. I'm coming down!'

He had heard. A sob rose in her throat. He had come looking for her. A scrambling sound, running footsteps—and Grant appeared, a giant shadow across the cave mouth, and saw her as she instinctively raised her arms in a gesture of appeal, cried out: 'Oh, help me, please!' and fell forward.

The next second she was in his arms as he knelt by her side, and his head was on her shoulder and she heard his muffled words:

'Thank God I found you!'

She was sobbing with relief, clinging to him, to the warmth of him, for she was freezing cold, and wet.

'My leg, I fell down the path—I think I've broken my leg, Grant——'

'Don't try and talk. Here, sit up a moment and drink this.' He helped her gently and then handed her a flask from his hip pocket. Even as she sipped the fiery whisky he was peeling off the warm jacket he wore.

'Oh, that's good. That is so good.' The whisky put life into her bones, filled her head with warmth so that she felt instantly better. He knelt again and began to ease off her mackintosh and coat.

'You'll have my jacket on. It's dry.'

'But you——' she protested weakly.

'Ach, I'm warm. Come now, don't argue with me.'

She wasn't strong enough anyway. She allowed him to put his coat on her, and was filled with his warmth immediately. 'Oh yes,' she breathed. 'That's better. Thank you.' It was no use. To her own alarm and dismay, she burst into tears.

He sat down beside her. Then gently, his arm went round her. 'Cry as much as you want,' he said. 'You are safe now. Safe with me.'

'Yes—I'm—I'm sorry to be such a baby——'

'Ach, no. After what you've been through? Are you well enough to tell me what happened?'

'Yes.' Haltingly at first, she began the tale of what had happened since leaving the house, and forgot her tears in the telling of it. And when she had finished, she asked: 'But how did you know where to look for me?'

'Do you know what time it is?' he asked very gently.

'About midnight?'

'It's nearly four o'clock in the morning. I have been all

over the island ever since I knew you'd gone—which was about half past eleven.'

'Oh! *Four*! But how—how did you know I wasn't in the house?'

'Edna told me she'd seen you going out for a walk, and of course, when the storm began she thought you'd be rushing back for your coffee—but you weren't, so—very diffidently —she mentioned it to me,. She didn't want to make a fuss over nothing, she said, but she felt I ought to know. Here's to the Ednas of this world,' he said, raising the flask before he took a swallow from it. 'But for her you'd have been here for God knows how long.'

'Oh. Yes. I must thank her.'

'And now, Miss Stevenson, I am going to take you to the nurse, to see what is wrong with you. And if your leg is broken, then we'll get the helicopter to take you to the mainland.'

'Yes,' she said. 'I'm—I'm leaving anyway on Tuesday.'

'I know.'

'You—know?'

'Yes. Jean spilt the beans when I called on them this morning—I mean yesterday, Sunday morning, to see if there was anything they needed. She was very upset with herself at letting it slip—but it was too late then.'

'Oh.'

'Why were you thinking of leaving, Lory?'

'Does it matter?' she answered. 'I paid my bill in advance, so it——'

'That's not what I meant,' he answered. 'I want you to tell me *why*.'

'No. Take me to the nurse's, please. I ache all over.'

'I know. So the sooner you tell me, the sooner we'll go.'

'I'm not starting a fight with you again, because you'd win hands down—so are you taking me or——' she stifled a sob—'you're—you're making me c-cry again——'

'Och, don't, please don't cry. I'm sorry, love, I can't fight

184

tears. I don't want to fight you either—I just wanted to know——'

'All right, I'll tell you,' she retorted, fighting back the treacherous sobs, 'it's because I don't want to stay on Creagdubh any longer with you around. In the words of that corny old phrase—this place ain't big enough for the both of us.'

'Because you detest me?'

'Yes—no—oh! Because you're a beast, and you're arrogant and rude and you don't like me, and you've made it perfectly clear, so I'm getting out of your way, so aren't you glad, and I'm still hurting all over but I'm feeling better every minute for being able to tell you what I really think of you——' the words were all tumbling out in mad confusion and she couldn't have stopped if she had wanted to, 'and after tomorrow—I mean, today—you're getting me all muddled now, I won't be here any more, so you can go around lairding it the way you want it, and not having to put up with nasty lady sociologists who *you* think want to tell you what to do and——'

She couldn't have stopped, but *he* silenced her very effectively by kissing her.

'What was that for?' she gasped.

'To shut you up, to tell you, as briefly as possible that I don't believe a word of what you've said, and also to say that I suspect you've been fighting certain feelings in yourself as much as I have. I wonder if you've failed as badly as I have?'

'What do you mean?' she asked in a very small voice.

'I mean, you little goose, that I discovered, when Jean told me you were planning to sneak away, that I loved you. That's all.'

'Oh!'

'Is that all you can say?' he demanded.

'Yes—no—oh!'

He began to laugh, then, very gently, turned her to face him. 'Kiss me,' he said. 'Then I'll know.'

185

There was no hesitation. And when, minutes later, they drew apart, he said softly: 'You're not leaving tomorrow. And if you do have to go by helicopter to the mainland, *I'm* going with you, so now you know. And I'm not letting you out of my sight, because one day soon, I'm going to marry you. Do you understand?'

'Mmm, kiss me again.'

Minutes later, as, rather reluctantly, they decided they ought to go, Lory said: 'Er—Grant, you're not going to believe this, but I saw—I *thought* I saw something rather odd just before you called me.'

He was helping her to her feet, holding her firmly so that she need not put her foot to the ground, apparently concentrating on his task, gentle and caring.

He paused, his arm round her very tightly. 'The Moon-dancers?'

'Yes. I know it was all my imagination—but honestly, they were very vivid——'

'Aye?' But there was something rather odd about his expression.

'You—you didn't see anything, did you?' she asked.

'Me? Ach, I've no time for that sort of superstition—you know me——'

'Did you?' she persisted.

'I'll tell you when we're married,' he answered. 'So you see, if you really want to know, you'll *have* to marry me, won't you?' And he swung her up into his arms and set off walking out of the cave.

'I have no choice,' she murmured. 'You promise you'll tell me?'

'Yes.'

And three months later, he did.